EVERYTHING UNDER
THE SUN

Everything under the Sun

AUSTRALIAN SHORT STORIES OF LIGHT AND SHADE FROM A TO Z

Ian Cochrane

Ingramspark

Contents

About this book and author

While there is lots of 'travel' in this Antipodean oddity of a book, the stories are very much focused on people, places and the human condition. The tales vary in length, a menagerie of the tall and the true, all intended to lead the reader to who knows where.

Wanderlust has lured Ian to The Americas, Europe, Asia and the South Pacific, with work taking him to India, Africa, Korea and the highlands of Papua New Guinea.

He has penned several books, including –

- Indian Summers – Mumbai and Beyond
- A World Away – Global Short Stories of Light and Shade from A to Z

His Australian Outback short story 'A Splendid Memory' was included among the 2013 non-fiction Cowley Literary Award finalists. There have also been several travel and food features published in The Australian.

Praise for the author

"Riveting as always, simply marvelous. Wonderful writing and so descriptive, your observation of detail is superb. An awe-inspiring landscape, brought to life with your usual descriptive flair" – Marty Rubin (USA), *Nothing Profound*

"I love the poignancy" – Brenda Addie (Australia), *All the World's A Stage*

"Well written; genuine and its rawness very effective" – Sandra Tyler (USA), *The Woven Tale Press*

"I have always wondered how you manage to transcend the reader to the very spot of action with but a handful of words – I guess it is some kind of magic you do, some voodoo" – Umashankar Pandey (India), *One Grain Amongst the Storm*

"Very moving, that last paragraph gave me chills" – Kris Landt (USA), *Channeling Hippocrates*

"Thank you, dear sir, for an abundantly rich shared moment in time" – Nickey Oosthuizen (South Africa)

"Bloody terrific. You traipse selectively through the mystical, reality, without disturbing the essence of history." – Ralph Jones (Australia), *Broowaha*

"Such a terrific writer. So much emotion and heartfelt feeling" – Phil (USA), *The Regular Guy NYC*

"I love the evocative atmosphere of your writing" – Guy Thair (UK), *The Wrong Stuff*

"Beautiful!" – Annie Boreson (USA), *Annie Off the Leash*

"What a wonderful word picture you paint" – Dennis Hogson (China), *The View from Fanling*

"A lovely descriptive piece" – Robert (USA), *Mulled Vine*

"Beautiful work. Great nuance and emotion" Janene Murphy (USA), *Enlightened: Light Vs Dark*

"Well written indeed – Thanks for another wonderful piece. Very touching" – Lanthie Ransom (South Africa), *Life Cherries*

"Poignant and beautiful" – Big D (UK), *Assorted Thoughts from an Unsorted Mind*

1

AT A VIKING FUNERAL – Daylesford, Victoria, 2013

I am 100km northeast of Melbourne. Boerne is 51 years old, handsome in a rugged sort of way; olive skin, high cheekbones and black straw-like hair. He has never been a talker and we sit on the veranda drinking beer instead, our eyes drawn to a 2x6m hired recycle bin out front. At the end of the day the sun is uncanny and low, the sky scarlet as summer bushfires rage in the western ranges.

"Good of you to help out," says Boerne, flicking the top from another beer. "To be honest, you know, I'd rather be somewhere else." And for the briefest of moments, his dark eyes leave the recycle bin. "Maybe we just got married too young. Who knows? In those days we just needed to get out." He passes me the beer. "Things were different then."

This is the second bin we have filled today, just there at the front door; clothes, doubled-up wedding and old birthday presents, books, magazines, the old couch Boerne's been sleeping on for weeks – and then there's the photo albums that neither Boerne or Ingrid want – all carried through the house and unceremoniously dumped in the bins. I stare at the 2-parked cars at the end of the house, side by side. I have not seen Boerne and Ingrid that close for years. It is still another hour before the truck arrives, and I walk inside for a leak.

They have been married for over 30-years these two, me having known Ingrid forever, with her mother living just next door to my father's place. "Is it a boyfriend?" her mother once asked me when Ingrid was late home the previous night. I said I didn't know. She was never brave enough to ask her own daughter about such things.

To me Ingrid was a normal teenager, mixing mostly with girlfriends after school. All three dressed in black when they went out; a cheeky mailman once glancing across at me before asking them, "Well girls, where's the funeral?" I remember watering the garden early one Sunday morning, with Ingrid rolling home drunk after quaffing half a bottle of gin. I helped her girlfriends smuggle Ingrid through her mother's back door.

And Ingrid was always pretty, so as it happened there was a boy. "Sure, you kidding? Of course he's nice!" she indignantly told me. "My height too." At 1.8m tall, Ingrid had a thing about that. "He's dark, and from the other side of town, thank goodness!" I wondered at the significance, and Ingrid screwed up her nose at my ignorance. "Really? Well it can't be as boring as around here!" I recall making a feeble attempt at looking hurt.

It was another three years before we next meet; her already married with a mother needing nursing due to a broken wrist. She asked about my travels, but unlike the feisty teenager I'd once known, seemed less forthcoming about herself. "Mum's a tough nut. I think she'll be fine. But, you know…none of us really talked, even when Dad was alive." I waited for something about her. "Me?" Ingrid laughs. "Work's just out of control."

From there on, I would catch up with Ingrid and Boerne each Christmas at her mother's place, where we'd chat casually over beer and burned sausages; pearls of weather wisdom, maybe work, and my tales of travel. Ingrid excelled in the world of insurance. Boerne moved from newspaper journalism to magazines.

To get from the bathroom to the kitchen I go over and around stacks of packed cardboard boxes, catching Ingrid leaning against a kitchen bench of polished granite. Ingrid is now 49 years old – looks 35 – loves the garden and in younger days excelled at most sports. Her hair is up in a bun, and her mascara smudged. She continues to stare outside the window until I wonder if she has forgotten I'm here. There is low sigh as her eyes wander towards me and settle. The traffic noise outside has stopped and Ingrid fumbles with her empty cup.

Finally, there's some light in her hazel eyes and she looks

towards the open front door, the overflowing recycle bin outside. "You know, they're not just leftovers; it's a part of my life…no, pieces of two lives we just break off and throw away." She talks in bursts, in fits and starts, as if waiting for me to approve or disapprove. "You know, we come and go, passing each other, between house and recycle bin. But I can't bare to look at his face or inside the bin. I feel strange, numb, my feet and head floating." I wonder if she'll cry. "Have I been treading water all this time?" She looks down at the floor, still holding the cup. Her knuckles are white. I am suddenly cold.

Her eyes lift. She takes a deep breath. "So…I suppose this is the funeral. Is there an afterlife?" I am caught in Ingrid's stare until, thank goodness, she again looks towards the front door. "You know, he still says almost nothing. I wonder if we ever really spoke at all."

Back on the veranda, I wait with Boerne for the truck to arrive to pick up the bins. I shield my eyes from a blazing sun as the truck turns into the driveway, pulls to a stop, the driver jumping out and fiddling with the remote to swing the boom. The last bin rises and drops onto the tray. The driver nods, no need to say anything.

As the truck moves off, there is a cough from the engine. A pall of black smoke hangs above the exhaust. One of the rear lights is not working. There is an eerie red shroud over everything now. The smell of smoke hangs heavy as the bins cruise down the street.

2

BEACHES AND BIRDSONG – Moreton Island, Queensland, 2017

The island is an odd shape – wide at the northern end, thinning down south – but at about 35km long it's the third biggest sand island in the world. We have been lucky to have previously spent time on Fraser Island, the largest, but are always on the lookout for something different.

The first we hear of Moreton is some weeks back in NSW, approached by the owners of a neighbouring camper trailer; John and Karen. They ask about our go-anywhere Troopy truck, John a butcher by trade. They have left their "now older kids at home to fend for themselves" and look for work here and there. Karen smiled. "Yeah, the money comes in handy, but life's not all about the money, is it?" There was butchering work to be had, and even an offer to manage a hotel for a couple of weeks... but I digress.

John had the words 'Moreton Island – escape the fake' emblazoned across the chest of his black tee shirt. "It's like Fraser," he said, "but quieter." So here we are on the Brisbane-Moreton ferry, after waking at 3:45am to catch the only ferry with any space – and a 5am departure – immediately dropping our tyre pressures to cope with the soft Moreton Island sand, before adjourning upstairs to gulp hot coffee and ponder the thought of our first 'serious' sand driving since Namibia over 2yrs previously.

Once on the Moreton beach there is a one-way track east, directly across the island, daunting sand hills at times, then narrow and winding, powder-soft, bumpy or deeply rutted. How one bloke tows a trailer is a mystery, and it's a welcome thought that we'll meet nothing from the opposite direction on this leg.

On our first day, an old timer warns that some get bored here. "Not much out 'ere mate... if you're not into fishin' that is. No possums, no kangaroos or koalas either... never 'ave been." He tells us tales of "blackfellas using local dolphins" to help with the herding of fish, and those first Australians living mostly off seafood. "And there are middens in track cuttin's mate, where the blackfellas had those feasts of shellfish... for thousands of years they did."

On the east coast our Troopy truck nestles among ocean coastal dunes with sublime sunsets, over a lagoon of a lake just a short walk inland – our camp with the constant roar of surf and the call of birds that flit and roost in the rolling surrounds of casuarina and banksia bush.

Our daily ritual starts with sunrise, a swim in the lake, the fresh water chilly, the air balmy but still. Next is breakfast: Innisfail red papaya, muscatels, banana and pot-set yogurt, the smell and taste of fresh-brewed coffee – hot and black – the last of a treasured gift all the way from Costa Rica.

Down by the surf the waves pound even louder. A pair of Brahminy Kites are white and russet red, flight feathers extended like fingers. They drop and soar on unseen thermals, and a stiff Pacific breeze laden with the smell of salt, where a single morning walk can last forever on this beach of a highway that is mostly empty, shiny and flat, with the gentle wash of surf.

From the beach we gaze south to the profile of Mt Tempest, the tallest vegetated sand dune in the southern hemisphere, then down the length of the coast until shrouded in sea mist, the weekend abode of long rods and wishful ocean fisherfolk that appear from nowhere, more like spirits than humankind.

Another sandy track leads across the bottom of the island back to the west coast and the sheltered waters of Moreton Bay, with Shark Point home to dugongs and giant turtles. From there we head north to where a distant lighthouse sits afloat a faded promontory in early morning light – an ancient Antipodean dreaming – or the maybe-memories of a Mediaeval Mont Saint Michel.

3

BEATING THE FLOOD – Diamantina, Queensland, 2017

'The Diamantina' channel country is 400km north of Birdsville, south-west Queensland, the surrounding landscape oddly akin to cowboy movies of the American Wild West. It is a day's drive, the season late spring, the sky a forever blue and the air smelling of dust.

Red rock outcrops are called 'jump-ups' in these parts; flat top, truncated, ancient mountain leftovers from some long-forgotten inland sea, seemingly sown at random across endless red plains with the scantest smattering of grey-blue bush. The channel country is a tangled, snakelike, labyrinth of dry waterways rutted and wrangled by past torrential onslaughts, the larger trees left with tangled, ancient roots laid bare on sandy riverbeds, with surrounding stony gibber plains and the occasional sink hole that lay in wait for unsuspecting adventurers that may be tempted to stray from the few established tracks.

So this is the mighty 'Diamantina' diaspora, the stuff of Outback verse, our truck rising and falling on a roller coaster of a road. Wayward cattle stare languidly, the land a rutted moonscape of a floodplain, with washed up flotsam pushed high in the canopy of these ancient stunted trees. The dry, scoured trenches flow wherever they wish.

Finally arriving at Hunter Gorge, we meet National Parks ranger Max tending the facilities and passing-on welcome weather details. "Yeah, some chance of rain I s'pose... but less chance than yesterday. Changeable country this, that's for sure." Those dark eyebrows are raised. "In my first year we were all stuck out at the homestead for months." There is a sweep of that giant hand in the rough direction of the old cattle station homestead we passed earlier on. "All you can see was flooded, for miles and miles and miles." Max pauses, could be only in his 20s, in faded green ranger garb, a mop of black hair under a wide-brimmed hat and the scant beginnings of a beard." He points down south, the old station homestead we remember being on the slightest rise, now the Parks office and accommodation. One of the few pieces of higher ground it seems.

Our camp overlooks a flotilla of pelicans cruising the coffee-coloured Diamantina water, fishing as one, upstream then down... floating this way, then the other, beaks down trawling, beaks up again... and on they go until dark. Our neighbour too catches fish, 5-yellow bellied perch within hours of arriving, and graciously offers us one; a delicious gift we wrap in foil with garlic and lemon slices, then leave to roast on our fire along with slices of saffron-coloured sweet potato that will melt in our mouths.

Later we listen to the ominous pitter-patter of rain for most of the night, recalling the ranger's earlier words, "Yeah, the isolation is kind of nice. But yeah, it can get tricky out here. You're a long way from anywhere and anyone I reckon." Max's eyes had narrowed to stress how serious things can get. "Even with 10mm of rain the roads get bloody impossible."

At 6am it's still dark as we lay in the top of our truck; a converted 2014 Toyota Land Cruiser Troop Carrier. It is still raining, but time to get up. We have decided to run for it, leaving those still sleeping in a scattering of vans and camper trailers. We don't fear the river – not for now anyway – but we do fear the notorious red mud.

We breakfast on fruit and yogurt in silence, still dark, wet drifts coming and going on a cool intermittent breeze, the smell of dust replaced by rain. Soles of our gumboots are layered in mud that seems more like glue, even though the ground is only wet on the surface, the sand still dry below.

We finish packing and rev up the truck with very first light, not daring to drive in the dark. There is no other sign of life. From our riverside campsite we slip and slide towards the gate, our tyre treads clogged with mud that was sand just yesterday... the truck in low range and 2nd gear. Olympic tobogganing on greasy mud comes to mind

Max had said "If you get to Brighton Downs, then you'll make it out." The window wipers settle into a rhythmic clap, our slicked-up tyres slip and slide, our truck barely missing a gate post. We are 70km from Brighton Downs, but are at least now out the gate.

It takes us over 2-hours to reach Brighton Downs, where we pause, take a deep breath and ponder the legendary amounts of water flowing through the Diamantina system in one 'normal' wet season, and the improbability of anyone driving out of here once the rain got serious. "2.4 cubic km a year" Max had said with some authority, "more than the water in all of Sydney Harbour."

4

BEYOND THE BLOOMFIELD – Cape Tribulation, Far North Queensland, 2017

It is a day's drive from Cooktown to the 537,000Ha Lakefield National Park, finally setting up camp at Horseshoe Lagoon, a serene patch of water covered in white lilies and a favourite haunt of brolgas, parrots and assorted waterbirds. At the end of the day we meet a group of twitchers camped across the way, having also arrived from Cooktown. "You've come from the south," they ask, eyebrows raised, "from the Daintree, then Cooktown?" We both nod. "You saw the accident on the Bloomfield?" Ah, no. We know nothing of any 'accident'.

Our neighbours are visibly shaken and tell us a vehicle travelling south towing a large trailer-van lost control on a downhill section of the Cowie Range. "You must have seen it!" The driver was badly injured, they tell us, the van and vehicle wrecked, with stunned onlookers sitting around while awaiting an ambulance. We look at each other but say nothing. As it happens, we did pass an ambulance travelling south that morning, but with no siren and no apparent urgency.

We spend a restless night, our sleep disrupted by wild pigs that grunt and slosh in the shallows just metres from our parked truck, us bothered by thoughts of the Bloomfield Track – with its river crossings and one particularly steep section through the Cowie Range – and us travelling that same treacherous section of the Bloomfield Track uphill, needing low 4WD and 1st gear, maybe minutes before the accident.

The next day we pick up some phone coverage briefly while travelling, a Google search confirming the injured driver was killed on impact. And weeks later at Laura – Far North Queensland, for the Queensland Cape York Aboriginal Dance Festival – a Daintree Parks Ranger tells us there have been 3-Daintree road fatalities in the last 2-months.

5

BIG BIRD BEACH – Etty Bay, Queensland, 2017

They call this the 'Cassowary Coast' and say it is the best place to spot these endangered beasties in the wild. So that's why we have come, to this tiny but beautiful alcove of a bay – just south of Innisfail, Queensland – with wet rainforest all the way down to the sea. And, as it happens, we have already passed one plain-looking juvenile on arrival, browsing by the side of the road in fading light.

There has been rain, with pools on the ground, mist on the far headland and tropical clouds black as we set up camp tucked in a corner between forest and beach, the heavy tropical air loaded with smells... that dank, often pungent mix of permanently wet leaf litter mulch, a multitude of living, breathing leaves in every shade of green and secret flowers we cannot see... and right here, the ozone rich sea mist, the surf and salt from the permanently pounding Pacific.

In the morning we wake to the drifting patter of rain on the roof. There's breakfast of fruit and yoghurt and the obligatory walk on the beach, this time in rain jackets, warm sand beneath bare feet, the air a balmy 24degC. But we are not alone it seems, met by a beach-going cassowary, a fully grown specimen this time – both sexes looking similar – resplendent in regal but hairy plumage of glistening black... bright blue neck with a splash of red, paler blue cheeks, dangling red wattles and the hallmark wedge-like crown, used to push a path through the thickest forest vines.

Later we receive another unexpected personal visit, and consider ourselves very lucky, this time at camp. There is the slightest pause, and we can't help feeling as though we are being sized-up, up close. That head is raised, turned then cocked, with gleaming, wizened eye... that mighty, clawed front foot paused mid-stride.

We look at each other. Is this the same bird we met earlier on the beach? But suddenly it's gone, having disappeared back into the seemingly impenetrable rainforest right next door, and we wonder if us human nomads all look alike to a beach-wandering cassowary.

6

BIRDS OF PARADISE – Perth, Western Australia, 2012

They sit in the kitchen – Mr and Mrs L – overlooking a backyard of woodpiles, wheelbarrows and tussocks of native grass. It is early summer. The pungent scent of rambling Chinese jasmine wafts across the yard and mingles with the smell of last night's rain. The weekend menagerie headcount is underway over fruit toast and espresso. Being Saturday, it will be hours before Little L, now 19, emerges to join the human race. Inheriting Mrs L's good looks, he is prone to late nights and a string of girlfriends.

At the rear of the yard the chickenhouse sits – `chookhouse'

in Aussie lingo – under giant lilly-pillies. Strings of bat-
tered prayer flags flutter 'tween boughs. Spotted turtledoves
coo and browse beside the newest acquisitions; three spoilt
chooks. Then there's the four moggies of varied ages, reclin-
ing in assorted pose, each in black-and-white tuxedos that
fool neighbours into thinking there's only one cat 'that gets
around a bit'.

Of the feathered newcomers, firstly there is Marie-Claire
the Belgian – a leopard-speckled breed called Mille Fleur or
'a thousand flowers'. A highly-strung watchdog with cute
whiskers, she warns the others of crows, or if a cat finds the
energy to raise a yawn. Then there are the almost-twins, both
fluff balls: Jane, a smoky lavender-grey, and Ebony, a shining
black beauty with a green lustre. Jane is the 'Labrador' of the
gang, the biggest glutton who loves a pat and a cuddle; seeing
any human as an opportunity, deftly cadging food from the
kind or unwary.

Ebony can be aloof, but prone to bouts of melancholy.
In the centre of the yard is a lemon tree and beneath it 'the
pen': an open wire cage propped on bricks, with ample food
and water. That becomes 'home' when she's taken with spells
of the dreaded 'black dog' – or 'broodiness' in chook lingo –
when she will refuse to lay and speaks in tongues; a continual
baritone 'cluck, cluck, cluck'. If left to her own devices, she
will sit flattened and fluffed in the laying box for days on end;
egg or no egg.

All three are bantams, with an inclination for multiple
breakfasts and large feathered hobbit's feet. They love a good
dust bath and seem intent on tunnelling to China. Marie-
Claire is short and sleek, with a thick neck and open tail

feathers like a geisha's fan. Both Jane and Ebony are Pekins, walking tea cosies with petticoats that billow in backyard breezes. These are all chooks of means – free-range girls – objecting vigorously and loudly, if left locked in their chook-house any later than 6am on any summer morning. And by a strange twist of fate, they all happen to share the names of Little L's past girlfriends.

Now it is noon, and Little L emerges from his upstairs lair. But, what's that? There is the pitter-patter of another pair of feet and an unfamiliar face appears from behind the door. "Oh… ahem… good morning," says Mrs L. Little L looks a trifle sheepish as he shifts from one foot to the other. "This is Jessica," he offers. Across the table Mrs L, peers bemused over the top of her glasses. "Well," says Mr L. "Does this mean we need another chook?"

7

——

BREAKFAST BANTER – Mary Kathleen, Queensland, 2017

This morning we ponder our breakfast bowls in quiet isolation, another milestone bush camp away from the road trains and caravans, about 100km east of Mt Isa, Outback Queensland... last night's neighbours a passing herd of camels with shining eyes, their footfalls the only sound on a balmy, starry night, Australia the only country in the world where it is still possible to see wild camels.

But it can be funny about breakfasts; the obvious things easily missed first thing in the morning, even after months on the road – with the dual milestones of 30,000kms and sharing over 100-breakfasts – we've just discovered our breakfast bowls are different, both being a valued parting gift from a friend. Yes, the bowls are exactly the same size... and yes... they are exactly the same colour. But hey, they are not the same. After all this time tagging them as either "the one on the right" or "the one on the left" – due to us having subtle differences in our breakfast preferences – we've found that one bowl has horizontal lines integrated into an otherwise similar pattern, whereas the other does not.

Oh, and those special breakfast dietary requirements? No, it is not about who likes ruby grapefruit, grapes, apple or apricot... or who does not. It's not about kiwi fruit or mandarin. And no, it's not even about the denomination of muesli or the dollop of yoghurt in each bowl. As it happens, we are both happy with all of the above.

But what it is about is the preferred banana proportion to be carefully placed in each bowl, and the degree of ripeness of said banana. Not so important? Well, that depends on how long you spend with someone – 24/7 being a long time – and it depends on who you talk to.

8

—

BROKEN BOARDS AND FADED DREAMS – Lara, Queensland, 2017

We are camped at Lara Station, 150km southeast of Longreach, Outback central Queensland. And to get to the homestead we've come through the 'back paddock' taking 2hrs to take the 10km cross country 'scenic route' on a puzzle of old government roads and muddy tractor tracks, opening and closing gates as we go. Scenic, yes, but definitely not the recommended route which happens to be via Landsborough Hwy.

We find the classic old Queensland homestead weather-worn and weary, but still grand, the rambling grounds deserted except for a friendly, well cared-for blue heeler at the gate of a modest, small cottage. A young woman camper is in a caravan out back of a larger shed. She looks surprised at the intrusion, wondering who we are. Yes, the owner Jo does live in the cottage, but is currently "out and about" and "the proper wetlands camping area is just down the road, with a caretaker on site".

Lara wetlands is a treed Eden, a large artesian pond littered with silent, brooding sentinels of bare, drowned trees, this spa and waterbird paradise all fed by the homestead bore since 1908. Tonight there is a pink dusky sky overhead, the smell of wood smoke from happy campers' fires and the goodnight calls of kookaburra, currawong and mudlark.

In the morning it's the musical trill of black and white pied butcherbirds. And today we finally meet the owner Jo – once a Sunshine Coast girl – having left home at 16yo to become an Outback mine driver/operator. At around 5'-6", she wears 'Western' garb, a blue shirt, well-worn boots and jeans, topped off by a tall, buff-coloured hat with a more than generous brim, crowned with resting sunglasses. The accent is country, measured but direct.

It is obvious from the start that Jo is the real thing, feisty and pragmatic, with steel-blue eyes, a dry sense of humour but an obvious affinity for others. And Jo is courageous, with not the slightest hint of any past misfortunes. As she tells it, she met and partnered Michael – a freelance helicopter pilot from a local family – first buying a station to the west, then moving home to here at Lara Station, a neglected 15,000 acre rambling cattle enterprise needing lots of love; the owner-builder having died an old man, leaving the son-in-law forbidden to enter, a dislocated family, and the old man's grand old timber-lined homestead forlorn and deserted for over 30yrs.

Jo stretches her wiry frame to her full height, with both thumbs tucked into her belt. "Yeah, it was a tall order, that's for sure. And times are tough 'round here... both the land and on the stations. We get the droughts and the floods, the whole box and dice... and in later days, even a mini-tornado that lifted the old place's roof."

But as well as the running of the station itself, and being of a practical bent, Jo had other ideas - a vision in fact - suggesting to Michael tourism's possibilities to augment the viability of the place. And with Michael often away flying for a week at a time, Jo finally convinced him that they should open up their property to travellers – grey nomads, assorted families and all that share a love of the bush and the great outdoors. Jo got to work, with Michael's help, putting her dream into action and with their very first camper arriving in 2014, a Swiss gent with accented English she hardly understood. But even though Jo was excited at the real beginning of their new venture – and spoke to Michael often whenever he was away flying – this time she kept the fantastic news secret.

A wistful smile escapes from the corner of Jo's mouth as she recalls the timing. "I decided It would be a nice surprise for Michael to see our first camper from the air, with Michael always flying in directly over the wetland camping area on his return home." There is a resigned shrug of Jo's shoulders,

Michael not making it home that night, his chopper crashing and her life partner Michael killed.

9

CALLING ON CANARVON – Canarvon Gorge, Queensland, 2017

Heading inland from Hervey Bay is a 500km detour from our previously planned coastal route north, and a big day's drive in most people's book. But we share the driving – and it is a World Heritage area after all – so what the hell!

We arrive at the National Park visitor centre in fading light, to find camping only allowed at specific times of year... with no camping just now. So we double back to just outside the Park boundary. We have happened across 'Sandstone Park', a sprawling cattle station dream of the owners, blessed with a high double ridge directly overlooking the gorge itself, although at the moment blanketed in drizzly black.

In the daylight, the weather is grey, cloudy with clearing rain. But the day ahead reveals some of the gorge's secrets, with a walk through the National Park over stepping-stone creek crossings to a natural amphitheatre reached via several flights of vertical steps, and a long chasm open to the sky while only a single person wide. A natural overhang is a gallery of indigenous painting on a vast, soaring sandstone wall, the onlooker feeling minuscule and irrelevant. Impossibly rock-wrought ponds and waterfalls are embellished with secluded moss gardens garnered with a dose of Dreamtime magic.

The evening brings a special bonus, gold-drenched sandstone escarpments, a roaring campfire and the smell of wood smoke under endless stars. On the second morning, the views are equally bewitching, of the same timeless escarpments – this time a dazzling white – among broken wisps of drifting mist, the calls of currawongs and cockatoos, and a visit from a lone bovine visitor looking bored with it all.

10

DAINTREE DREAMING – Daintree, Far North Queensland, 2017

As it happens, I have been here before... to The Daintree that is. And it is a bit odd, to travel back in time as much as 30yrs, when a piece of the puzzle seems to be missing. I remember a resort right here... somewhere... a glorious concoction of timber, of walkways and treehouses, surrounded by jungle straddling a tarred road that peters out to a 4WD track eventually reaching Cooktown, then Cape York; locally known as 'The Tip'.

But here we are, me with a fading, almost-mythical memory of a place that may never have existed at all. And it is only after several trips up and down the road, that we find an overgrown, partly-obscured sign on the side of the road, a once-stylish, fluorescent sign, now washed-out and broken.

On the beach side of the road is what's left of the cafe, bar, 2-pools now of the brightest green and gift shop, timber walkways and drive through, now broken, rotting and engulfed by this voracious world-famous rainforest, the air alive with morning birdsong and awash with the rush of nearby waves on golden sand. Up the mountain is the accommodation, what is left of once-glorious treehouse lodges. There too are the ruins of a grand reception and restaurant, windows crooked and broken, many timber steps and much of the deck rotten. Jungle vines hang, ferns smother and choke, but we push on through. Trees and palms sprout in sodden tropical air, the smell of bats thick, the rampant foliage always damp, eagerly reclaiming its own, and the dreams of all that passed this way.

The first owner's vision was to create something special here, The Daintree already special... something special memories are made of, a realized dream that lingers and stays with all that are lucky to have visited here. But now we stand in a heavy, humid midday silence, the ghostly echoes of guests' footsteps long, long gone.

It seems this `Coconuts Resort' dream was abandoned years back, eventually beaten by the regular, unrelenting, dreary wet seasons – and the absence of guests – finally surrendering to financial ruin and liquidation. Then followed a sequence of dreamer-owners eventually also leaving this place deserted, forlorn and empty, at the mercy of the engulfing Amazonian greenery while ensuring the place is even more special as is the way of lost cities and abandoned dreams.

11

A DANCE IN TIME – Laura, Far North Queensland, 2017

From Cape York we have driven south to Laura – not to be confused with nearby 'Old Laura' or 'New Laura' – and we are here for the 2017 bi-annual Aboriginal Dance Festival, our Laura an outback town with a population of 80 and a pub with Chinese backpacker staff that serves barramundi and beer, with space for campers out back. There is a post office doubling as a general store, a caravan park and tourist information centre.

But it is just to the south of here that things get special... with the world-famous Aboriginal Quinkan Aboriginal rock art going back thousands of years, including striking depictions of emus, kangaroos, human figures and the ever-present spirit world. And further south is a dedicated bush camping ground surrounded by a natural rock amphitheatre where the dance festival is held.

And this year's festival has special significance for us, being just back from 'The Tip', and now with some knowledge of the participating Cape York Aboriginal communities that include Mapoon, Bamaga and Lockhart River, all being isolated Australian Cape communities of which we were previously unaware.

Our favourites are the Lockhart mob, having visited the area on our way north to the tip of Cape York, and having been lucky to later meet 2-teachers talking of leaving their current positions at a Brisbane city school to embark on "more challenging, more rewarding roles"... at Lockhart River as it happens. We are camped next door at Elliot Falls when we first meet on the Old Telegraph Track, and after a swim to wash off the dust are kindly invited around to share their fire.

Steve is aware of the gravity of their decision, but they are both "looking for a change after almost 30-years in the system". He pauses to collect the right words, looks across at his partner Karen and adds. "We really would like to make a difference, and we think we can do that." He pokes at the fire. "I'm told the big thing is to get the kids to school in the first place, and then to create opportunities for them that make coming to school a more appealing option than not coming". He then adds " We hope to go there and be good role models for the kids." Steve looks pensive, and Karen nods agreement. We are impressed. Steve is a big guy, looks fit, and both Steve and Karen are eloquent and impassioned. I am sure they'll be a formidable combination, a great help to the Lockhart community and the school principal whom they have both known since the late 80's when they first met in Canberra.

At Laura the dance festival is in full swing, with the Lockhart River mob currently going through their paces. And it is obvious they are the favourites in our part of the crowd, especially with a woman in a wide-brimmed hat – the school Principal we are later told – standing behind us, her shouts enthusiastic, loud and encouraging… and suitably biased.

We are struck by the age mix of these Lockhart dancers, tiny kids of around 2yo, teenagers and older dancers too. One Elder wears glasses and has an intercom unit strapped to his belt. Another is a middle-aged woman with wide eyes, wild grey hair and very animated... all with the traditional paint, grass skirts and the totemic moves of their clan. And we are struck by the rhythms and chants, the gasps and cheers of the mixed crowd... the hypnotic click of clapsticks and boomerangs.

12

DARKSIDE DOWNUNDER – Hobart, Tasmania, 2015

I am in Tasmania drinking with Dave; a giant of a man with broad shoulders and no neck. He has lived alone all his adult life, and sits at his normal spot at the bar, in brown flannelette shirt and singlet, jeans and mud-caked Blundy boots. "Changed? Yeah, sure has mate." He looks around. "Mmm... not sure what me old mum would think!"

Dave's first pint "doesn't touch the sides", and he wipes the froth from his mouth. "Been to MONA?" I nod. His eyes wander to the window. "Mmm... to be honest mate... it's a bit confronting." He is "old school Tassie born and bred", his father a possum trapper, lost in a freezing Central Plateau blizzard in "a shocker of a winter." Dave was only 10, his mother "doin' it tough" and dying young. These days he "gets about a bit" having sold off most of the potato farm. He looks up from his beer. "I've been to London you know… and like a good museum." He gazes over the road and water to MONA's walls and rusted ramparts. "Not sure about MONA but."

My own first visit to MONA was in 2011, at the end of a southern summer, and with the museum newly opened: a chameleon collection of art set in an architectural creation on a bold scale – the 'Museum of Old and New Art' – and the realised sectarian vision of David Walsh with the help of Australian architect Nonda Katsalidis.

Once named 'Australia's top art collector' by BRW magazine, Walsh made his money from gambling, developing a highly technical system with computer-geek friends. He has, he says, a gift for mathematics… and outrageous luck. Once, having too much cash when about to fly home from Europe, he exchanged cash for ancient coins, thereby adding to his already considerable collection. After another overseas foray and returning with an Egyptian mummy, Walsh was asked to supply a death certificate.

I recall a MONA attendant pointing to a solid door. "Only 2 allowed at any one time please… and do keep to the path when inside", she advises. Inside it is inky dark and ominous: an oppressive vacuum of silence. The narrow white path stops, my girlfriend's breathing somewhere behind me.

Stepping stones are low, flat and square, surrounded by black: "real water" we've been warned. I am momentarily off-balance as I reach a 90deg turn: a single round stepping stone directly below a stark face morphing from a black wall. The face emerges; just one dark eye, a heavy eyelid and long lashes. The pale, translucent skin has freckles – is oddly unsettling – uneven nostrils and pearly-white teeth under a pink upper lip. A white shroud hides the other eye and lower lip. We have been transported to a morgue.

I turn in the gloom, the steps again square, dragging my gaze away from that face now behind me; acutely aware of that vacant unsettling stare, and my girlfriend's unsteady steps following in the darkness. Ahead are two white obelisks: on my left a sealed Egyptian sarcophagus, to the right Walsh's now legendary Egyptian mummy. I'm startled as the mummy's magical wrapping dissolves before my eyes, revealing ancient red tissue and skeleton; Walsh having commissioned the local Hobart Hospital to provide the photographic scans.

On that first visit to MONA, we have caught a ferry from the city to the Moorilla Peninsula and descended a glass circular lift at MONA, down 17m into a bunker with a well-appointed bar; ornate antique chairs in lush multihued velvet "for sitting on, not just for show": a Walsh instruction.

20-something Dan is friendly and enthusiastic, as are all attendants, in their black tailored, ragged-edged uniforms. Dan assures us the stupendous walls of rough-hewn sandstone are "the real thing; the entire Moorilla peninsula made of the stuff."

We are handed iPods locating exactly where we are and any nearby displays, along with all the background we need, including 'art wank' reviews. We tap 'like' or 'hate' on the touch screen; our opinions kept for posterity. A waterfall spray cascades down a sheer sandstone rock face, the light and droplets forming the top Google words of the moment, all on high rotation. A row of filing cabinets are not the normal office variety – nothing's normal here: a vertical bank of more than 50-drawers, each with the blink of a life inside; on the front of each drawer, a small 3-D face: a bank of peering orange faces, each willing me to choose just one. I grip the handle and pull, surprised by a baby voice: "I love you", repeated over and over; the open drawer revealing a black plaque with an engraved poem. The faces and disembodied voices are all different, the written words a dedicated poem, romantic and poignant – some achingly so.

Along a cloistered corridor, we are met by MONA's most provocative displays in semi-darkness: an array of human anatomy, the distorted, forlorn form of a dead horse hanging from a rope, and the chocolate-moulded half torso of what is left of a hooded suicide bomber. There is something unsettling about having to choose to give yourself a 'lethal injection' while sitting in a dimly-lit room on a comfortable lounge chair.

In the gloomy environs I lose my girlfriend more than once. There are no labels, no descriptions, no fences, no ropes or barricades. We're dwarfed by Sidney Nolan's 1620-panel, multicoloured 'Snake', winding its 45m way through the main gallery. A machine mimics the full gamut of human digestion, and an oddly obscene 'fatcar' Porsche with black leather seats and gleaming red panels bloated and on the verge of bursting. A giant earth-like disc hangs from the wall; a Damien Hirst spin painting with a mysterious inner glow.

On the floor below are 2 penguins in earnest conversation, the taller with head tossed back, beak open wide; a reassuring flipper thrown over the shoulder of his companion.

Another display pays homage to the mystery of numbers, maybe a nod to Pythagoras (or could it be Walsh?): to those magician-mathematicians of yore and a mystical binary system that uses only the numbers `1' and `0'.

The vibrating hum of some secret transformer invades the senses as I wind along a rectangular labyrinth, between grey walls covered in the hypnotic forms of binaries, until I stoop under a low lintel to reach the dark heart. I enter the cramped space and instinctively look up, startled by the roof appearing to fall on my head; my unexpected reflection, complete with my glowing MONA iPod in hand.

The doors are already closed to late arrivals; attendants begin to muster, readying themselves for day's end. Outside we linger among high rusty ramparts on an elevated patio by a full size concrete mixer made of rusty iron lacework by an eclectic Belgian artist. Dan has an aunt who worked for the first Moorilla owner Claudio Alcorso. He stops as he passes, his gaze taking in the Derwent and his straddling city of Hobart. "Alcorso? Sure..."Dan sits his a leather shoulder bag on the grass. "...be happy to help. It all starts with Claudio establishing Moorilla vineyards in 1958". I exchange glances with my girlfriend, with her not even born. "Yes, many years back now; Claudio having fled a fascist Italy in the 1930s. Interesting that after that, he was interred during WWII." Dan shrugs. "Afterwards he moves a successful textile business to here, of all places he could have gone." I wonder aloud at the choice and Dan scratches a newly sprouting moustache.

"A visionary? For sure", says Dan, "a passionate patron of the arts and really, the father of the wine industry down here."

David Walsh buys the property in 1995, then an operating winery, and creating 'Moorilla Museum of Antiquities'– housing his private collection of South American artefacts, Roman mosaics and African tribal art. He soon realises visitors are more interested in the wine; MONA construction starting in 2007.

Dan points to the foot of the steps and we stare; Walsh having arrived in a shiny 4WD and is bounding upstairs with a hound the size of a small pony; Walsh's grey-streaked hair streaming behind him in the freshening wind.

That night we relax a Katsalidis cabin named Roy; with all accommodation named for architects and artists – in this case another Australian architect: Sir Roy Grounds. At breakfast we overlook manicured green to an open stage….and Walsh walking the dog. I see a confident man; not the reported misfit nerd of a kid from the shadow of Mt Wellington and working-class Glenorchy, the youngest of three siblings who went on to become a university dropout, broke at age 25.

Dave is up to his third pint, the pub almost empty. I am pondering the immensity of MONA just over the road: sad, beautiful, breathtaking, romantic, enlightening, inspiring, visionary, funny, shocking; or is it just plain gross? I am thinking all of the above, with a dash of the dark, the ominous and mysterious.

And I wonder about Walsh, and when the man first mooted this grand idea, having had the vision, the courage to see it through, not burdened by the personal criticism from the establishment, or the notion of whether visitors liked or disliked the displays. I do agree with Dave though. MONA can be confronting.

13

DOWN IN THE LUCKY COUNTRY – Melbourne, Victoria, 2015

Straight from a long lunch, I raised my umbrella and headed for the pedestrian bridge. Crossing the river, I turned onto the station path; Melbourne cold and soaked after 6-days rain. I recall the soulful sounds of an upright 2-string Vietnamese fiddle commingling with the distant strains of bagpipes that echo from under the bluestone bridge. There is the flash of a tram – all green and gold – the city-bound clatter and the clang of a bell. Looking at my watch, I have shaken the umbrella and turned to drop down the steps, I scan my ticket after dodging smokers engrossed in that final cigarette; the bang of the rotating barricade rebounding on tunnel walls, me passing busy office workers pushing in the opposite direction. At the foot of my platform up-ramp something stirred; a dark shadowed mound, commuters by-passing in the gloom.

Moving closer, I stopped short of my ramp. A hooded, stooped vision sat, a man I guessed, jacket back against the subway wall, surrounded by bulging plastic bags; blanket-wrapped knees pulled up under a stubble chin, and an ancient upright shopping trolley, tartan canvas ripped and miss-matched wheels. I took the extra steps to drop some coins by the cup, before stepping back and rushing on and up the ramp. Once at the top I paused. Peering up at the board, I have missed my train, but really was not bothered, preoccupied with thoughts of the man in the tunnel below. I asked the platform attendant.

"Yeah mate, I know who you mean." He shook his head. "Don't see him much though; reckon he's about 18. We call him Brian." I must have looked surprised. "Yeah, we give them all names. New faces every day `round here. You know… I reckon there's thousands of 'em. They could fill a football ground with the homeless here!" His eyes narrowed in thought. "How can that bloody-well be?" He again paused, scratched his chin and twisted the corner of his mouth. "I've no idea where Brian goes at night. Someone sees him across the road at St. Pauls when it's really cold; chasing some soup I s'pose." He pointed up the platform. "But I reckon he sleeps in the rail yards. He don't like the refuges, reckons they're unsafe and there's no privacy. So he moves around a bit."

I stared back down the bustling ramp to the tunnel at the commuters surging up and down.

Today it is almost 12-months since standing on that same covered platform with Brian sheltering below, me again wandering the great cities of Europe and the cultural smorgasbord of New York. But I am 'home' for now, lucky to reside in a city of my choosing, and immersing myself in the largest cultural event in Australia, the Melbourne International Comedy Festival, but there is also the eclectic live music that brings me back; the architecture, film and theatre. There is sport too, if you are that way inclined. And yes, there are the people of course, dressed in ubiquitous tones of Melbourne black.

But here on the platform, there is a lingering image that has somehow returned; a darker side of the urban dream. It is memories of Brian's half-hidden face that bothers me, down there in the subterranean gloom; where oblivious city-goers rush and stumble past, Brian half hid in his heaps of plastic. I can't see his eyes but suspect the light is already dimmed, despondent with chin on knees, bare hands grey, knuckles white; a small plastic cup, empty and on its side, my loose coins scattered, shining but inconsequential. I still see him sitting on the damp concrete, bent knees pulled up; a grubby envelope, flat on the wet ground, smudged words in pencil by a shaky hand: 'HELP PLEASE

I stare out across the rail yards and into the rusted jungle of tracks and posts. I am stuck with that thought of Brian, still sleeping rough, lugging his meagre belongings and heading into another Melbourne winter. I zip up my Gore-Tex jacket and lift my eyes from the rail yard maze, to the distant tiers and light towers of the Melbourne Football Ground; the 1853 'MCG' being the home of Australian Rules football and considered an iconic world sports venue with capacity for 100,000 fans.

But I'm thinking about Brian, and it seems appropriate that today – on the 18th April – the Melbourne City Mission hopes for 1500 willing souls to pay $60 a head to rough-it; for the privilege of bedding down under the stars in the hallowed MCG concourse, and to help end youth homelessness. The ticket includes a beanie, pillow and a cardboard box to sleep on. There are bread rolls, soup and a meat pie for dinner. In the morning, breakfast is a muffin, with tea or coffee. I am sure Brian would approve – if he is still with us – especially if offered a quiet seat somewhere off to the side, along with a muffin.

The train pulls in with a rumble, my mind wandering to the plight of 105,000 homeless in this 'The Lucky Country' of 24-million, and the results of yet another survey awarding Melbourne the 'Most Liveable City in the World'; along with the hopeful words of the UN Universal Declaration of Human Rights –

'Everyone has the right to a standard of living adequate for the health and well-being of themselves and their family, including food, clothing, housing and medical care and necessary social services, and the right to security in the event of unemployment, sickness, disability, widowhood, old age or other lack of livelihood in circumstances beyond their control.' I wonder how the rest of the less-lucky world is doing.

14

FELINE OF THE OPERA – Melbourne, Victoria, 2013

Outside there is a neon finger-sign soaring skyward, the oversized letters reading `ASTOR'. The building's not much to look at; the high facade brick, of cream and red. The veranda is low and squarish, the fascia lined with a string of bare light globes. From a street clogged with trams, trucks and cars, we step up and push through the bank of glass doors.

The door swings shut behind us; the clatter of traffic replaced by ambient music and dimmed lighting. We have been transported from a mad Metropolis into an art deco opera house. The grand foyer is ship-like in warm beeswax tones; a colonial ocean-going liner afloat on orient seas. A scattering of large potted palms sit on shining terrazzo floors.

I am inside Melbourne's iconic Astor Theatre with my girlfriend; classic 1930s, with a single-screen, stalls and a dress circle. In continuous operation, this is the last of its kind here. But even more important, I'm told it's the domain of Marzipan the cat. From the foyer I peer up into a huge oval opening in the upper floor, a pink ceiling and central chandelier. On the far side, a grand terrazzo staircase leads upwards, parting flights sweep left and right. The ticket box window glows at the foot of the stairs. A long wooden counter lines one side wall and we thumb through theatre flyers and calendar programmes stacked on top. Oversized wall posters are glazed, mounted in ornate gilded frames.

We buy tickets from the seller, tucked-in behind her desk and surrounded by posters, then climb the steps. My fingers run along the smooth wooden balustrade and we step onto a carpet awash with splashes of geometric colour. There is a wicker basket and cushion by the wall; Marzipan is not home.

Club chairs and sofas sit beneath framed posters, among further pots of palms. Dark sideboards are bedecked with tall vases of flowers. We walk to the balustrade, peer over the rail and down through the oval opening to the foyer now below us. Around the walls there are antique theatre projectors, radios and cinematic memorabilia. A grand piano sits off to the side. Rita Hayworth looks down from a wall, an amazon vision with flaming red hair and flowing dress of baby blue; a white stole is draped at her feet. I smell coffee and popcorn from the bar. There is champagne, beer and homemade cake, along with the best choc-tops in town.

We have met Mathew, a photographer friend, and sit talking on a sofa. It's Monday, a quiet night, with a Hitchcock double of Psycho and The Birds. Mathew is a long-time patron. "Marzipan? Of course." He looks around. "She'll be somewhere about." We have been here before, but have never seen the famous cat. Mathew picks up on my girlfriend's pout. "Never mind, she is her own cat, that one."

Marzipan is over 20yrs old; enjoying the same fame in these parts as a Scarlett Johansson or Penelope Cruz. And – being a cat – Marzipan is not bothered by any perceived contradiction between feline aloofness and allowing hundreds of doting patrons to offer food and blankets. And it only adds to the legend how Marzipan magically appears when called for dinner, even though stone deaf. "You know," says Mathew, "she once scared the hell out of an audience during a screening of Poltergeist, by running along the balustrade at an inopportune moment."

Before the film, I ask Mathew where it all began. "Ah, there's a story," he says, "she waltzed in as a kitten, from under a parked truck. Still occasionally goes outside. These days she's more likely to leap from the darkness during a movie and onto a lap of her choosing." I look over at my girlfriend, worried about the famous Hitchcock shower scene we are about to sit through.

My girlfriend asks if Marzipan likes horror movies. Mathew shrugs. "Well, you may laugh; but she does have a preference for some films over others." I ask Mathew what they would be and he does not blink an eyelid. "Oh, she likes some Tennessee Williams; and anything with Cat Woman of course."

We present our tickets and make our way up more steps into the auditorium, dropping the folded swinging seats with a bang. They are leather and squeak when we sit. The music stops and there is the grind of the winch as the gold curtains part. I spend most of the film peering into the shadows and around the seats, my girlfriend jumping at the crunch of a choc-top and the rustle of a chip wrapper. Another seat bangs in the gloom as someone jumps up, then trips on a step.

We stay for the credits, but alas, no Marzipan. I look down into the stalls far below. The theatre is gigantic, with downstairs generally closed off. She could be anywhere among the 1150 seats. She could be backstage, or up in the ceilings. Could she be outside counting traffic or just watching the world go by? Oh well, there is the second feature still to come.

At the end of the night we sit by the bar and chat. Eventually we trudge across to the top of the main staircase – the wicker basket still empty – then down to an almost empty foyer. There is someone pointing; towards us it seems. Mathew nudges my arm and we turn around. Marzipan has materialised from parts unknown and sits bolt upright, behind us on the terrazzo landing; resplendent in a tuxedo of calico tortoiseshell, white feet demurely together. Her purple and gold nametag hangs from a collar of lipstick-red. Mathew smiles at my girlfriend, "There you go. Where would a diva cat wait, other than on the exit stairs at the end of the night?"

Marzipan looks through us, then left; a bare wall obviously more interesting. Finally, those wise pool-like eyes gaze down at my girlfriend's feet. "So," says Mathew, "meet Marzipan, the phantom cat with 500 Facebook friends and a collection of `wish you were here' holiday postcards from all over the world."

15

GHOSTS AMONG THE STONES – Cobourg Peninsula, Northern Territory, 2017

From Kakadu and the East 'Alligator' River it is a 4-hour drive to Cobourg Peninsula's 'Caiman' Creek, although it's anyone's guess what those two reptiles have to do with Australia's Northern Territory... the drive beginning with an East Alligator crossing where the causeway is partially blocked with waiting saltwater crocs – not alligators – the 2m to 4m beasties ignoring our truck as they wait for tidal change and the unsuspecting fish that follow. At Caiman Creek we are

550km east and slightly north of Darwin, getting here via a badly corrugated road, lined with bush and narrow at times.

The region is part of West Arnhem Land, returned to Aboriginal ownership in 1981, having first arrived around 40,000yrs ago and more recently seeing outsiders come and go... Indonesian sailor-traders, buffalo and croc hunters, pearlers, missionaries, tourists and fisherfolk of all denominations. And it is just south of here that was thought a good place for a European settlement in the 1830s, even without a convenient supply of fresh water, an initial survey conducted at the end of the wet season and the British colonials being preoccupied with a perceived threat of Dutch and French expansion in the region.

A 43m long jetty was built, but wrecked by a cyclone the following year. A prefabricated building intended as 'Government House' was lifted off its stone pillar foundations and dumped 3m away.

Within 6-years the settlement was struggling, with half the garrison, initially from Tasmania, crowded into the small hospital suffering from malaria... along with scurvy, influenza, dysentery and diarrhoea. And it is the ruins of 'Victoria' we are here to see, a 6-hour round trip by boat only, including a 4km hike round the site.

Our guide is Travis, initially from South Australia, maybe 40, with a tangle of dark wind-tussled hair tied in a ponytail, a long-sleeved fishing shirt, football shorts and bare feet. Travis is well read, has worked "in mental health with Central Australian indigenous communities", and has been a tour guide in the Kimberley, Kakadu and Tasmania. These days he is based here, "married with family and a mortgage."

The first thing we see is a 20m high cliff, red and white, with what's left of the jetty below. Travis noses the boat into the shallows and on to the white sandy beach. He grabs a 1-ltr bottle of water... and an epirb; our emergency locating device. "The most important thing we have on board I reckon." He smiles. "Pretty damn isolated out here."

We look around, what is left being stone, the ruins including a powder magazine still intact, and what is left of the married quarters with Cornish-style round stone chimneys. There are also the ruins of 2-Quartermaster's stores, a blacksmith's, limestone kiln, hospital, kitchen and bake house.

The cemetery is a quiet, forlorn place, dominated by a handful of graves including that of an Italian priest who chose to live with the local Aborigines instead of within the settlement, and over on the edge of the jungle a tall stone spire dedicated to the wife of the longest-serving officer, Lieutenant Lambrick, his 40 year-old Emma the much-loved matriarch of the settlement who died during childbirth in October 1846.

Travis is quiet for moment. "Yeah, that was tragic really. But it seems the settlement limped along for another 3-years, 'till the sickness and death of both the Assistant and Chief Surgeon... the last deaths recorded here."

Travis shrugs. "Mmmm... odd that one... both the Assistant and Chief dying in the same year I mean."

The late morning glare is intense, and Travis' eyes narrow. "The books tell us they failed here due to ambitious trade hopes not eventuating." I must look doubtful considering the population never exceeded 70 souls. Travis smiled. "Well yeah, I know... they'd hoped that Victoria Settlement could be another Singapore... way out here. But supplies, were unreliable and infrequent, storing stuff in this climate difficult... I mean half the flour weight was weevils! And there was of course the disease, and the wild but mostly oppressive weather."

"They did have a garden I suppose, but the soil is not so good up here, and anything harvested was mostly eaten by rats. And malaria was the major killer here, spread by mosquitoes of course... but they never got what it was about." Travis shook his head. "The Aboriginal mobs knew it was mosquitoes that carry malaria. They took preventative steps, like using smoke, and smearing clay on their skin. But the Brits thought malaria was caused by bad air."

Travis has one child, with another baby on the way. He frowns, then gazes out to sea. "No kids made it through here, and I reckon the real reason the place failed was that it died of a broken heart, with the death of Emma Lambrick... and her baby, Emma having already lost her only son the previous year.

"I often wonder what happened to Emma's husband, that Lieutenant Lambrick, him being second in charge and the longest serving officer here at Victoria Settlement until finally abandoned in 1849... him losing everything after being stuck here for 11yrs."

16

GRIM BY NAME BUT NOT BY NATURE – Cape Grim, Tasmania, 2016

We overnight on the car ferry from Melbourne to Davenport, the treacherous Bass Strait an ominous black chop. With an early dinner and a cosy twin cabin our morning port of Davenport lay sleepy and cold. By midday we're driving 180kms to the west, the most northwest point of Tasmania, with an annual rainfall of almost 1m and according to one of only 3 'Baseline Air Pollution Stations' on the planet `The cleanest air in the world'.

We've passed rolling green fields of wind turbines, over 50 of the gangly beasts producing 12% of the state's power;

each 60m tall, with rotors the span of a Boeing747 and generator housings as big as a bus. Next it is the old Van Dieman's Land Company homestead, once a great wool empire. There is a deserted shearing shed and echoed footsteps from a dust-laden floor. There are rambling shearers' quarters and a gap in a dark row of cyprus wrent by a recent tornado, miraculously leaving the old kitchen intact, the photos of black folk with missionary garb and blank bewildered stares.

And finally we are up here on the coast, the goal of our journey; buffeted by fresh salty air and the crash of grandiose southern oceans. To the south lay the Antarctic. To the west, the famed 'Roaring 40s' winds, blown all the way from Argentina past the southern tip of Africa to get here; those same gales lashing our faces. We have wool and possum fur beanies pulled down tight, flapping Goretex jackets all buttoned up. I wonder at the wrecks that must surely be buried in paddocks of kelp that sway on sub-sea tides.

We gaze northward, to a tall natural rampart topped by rich green grass, grey and white waves crashing at its base. This is 'Suicide Bay', where a band of the local Pendowtee Mob were shot in 1828, their bodies thrown over the edge of the 60m precipice; the culmination of a series of events beginning with the harassment, abduction and rape of Pendowtee womenfolk.

So we really are at `Cape Grim', evocatively named by the intrepid English navigator and cartographer Matthew Flinders, from his 8m open whaling boat... for the wild weather and bitter winds, the huge swells, hissing foam and boiling cauldron seas, or maybe the treacherous rocky reefs... or could it really have been named in honour of a Mr 'Grim'?

There are flashes of sun on shining seas, the salt and spray a timeless presence. Broken clouds race on eastward, shedding shadows dark, on grassy tussocks and rolling pastures painted in hues of emerald green.

17

HARD TIMES IN DOGTOWN – Cape Arnhem, Northern Territory, 2017

We are 1000km east of Darwin, our only access to here via the Central Arnhem Road, arriving at the turnoff late afternoon. Then it is still another 20km off the main track, with compulsory vehicle restrictions fair warning: *"Vehicle must be 4WD with plenty of clearance, 2m max width x 2-1/2m max height."*

On the descent from the escarpment the scrub crowds in, the sand deepens, tree roots and the occasional drift of rock add to the chance of a puncture. Our first glimpse of the water is between 60m dunes, the sand deeper and softer here.

Our truck turns into a roller coaster, the steeper crests topped with slats of wood tied together and laid across the track to help with traction. Many of the connections are broken, with some slats impaled in a mess of white sand. Finally, we choose a path just above the beach waterline, the tide retreating for the next couple of hours. We pass the sacred site of Twin Eagles, impressive pieces of rock joined to the mainland by sandbars. This is a wild coast, isolated and often windswept.

Our camp lay between stands of bull oaks where the slightest breeze sounds like the rush of a river, the ocean waves a constant wash, a timeless ebb and flow. A pair of osprey fish offshore and sooty oystercatchers wander wet sand. There are dingo footprints for the length of the beach. They seem small and delicate, their direction straight.

We meet Ron the fisherman, a tradie from Darwin. He fishes alone from the rocks here, has 5-rods and has "been here 4-times now." He has dark hair tied back in a ponytail and swims fully clothed in his shirt and jeans, "to cool off after lunch" he says. "Have seen some crocs, but never a dingo till now." Ron has no time for dingoes. "You seen the damage those buggers do?" He wipes loose strands of his wet hair away from his face. "Yeah, this one, she's small... probably has pups somewhere. They'd call her a fox down south."

On our first night any breeze is soon gone, the sea a breathing lullaby, the early evening a welcome relief from the normally sweltering sun. The full moon is late rising, finally lighting the dark, hilly landscape where our truck is nestled.

The next morning we lay low in the shallows, the tide out, the sun already hot. There is no sign of crocs. The dingo approaches from the fisherman's camp, stops and stares, not 5m away... then takes a measured step even closer, her delicate front paws now in the water. She is young, with a fine white muzzle and black nose. We can see her ribs, but her sand-red coat is clean, unmarked by mange or scars. She sniffs the air and stares, her eyebrows white, those eyes brown and questioning, "Are they dangerous? Are they food... maybe some beached animal that could be dinner?" Her cautious curiosity is tangible, before she finally turns, gives us one last look, then resumes her business-like trot, off and down the beach before turning at some rocks, then disappearing up into the dunes.

That night we cook pork on the campfire, the fireplace a rusted steel ring in the sand, our burning logs within, half the top a cast steel grate. Early morning we finish coffee and there is movement in the corner of my eye. Then all is still by the makeshift BBQ. She stands as if frozen, neck stretched and nose towards the now cold grill, those eyes watching us. But the pork steaks are long gone, just a memory of last night's dinner with a bottle of Italian red wine, a dash of garlic and a kale salad with shredded Parmesan cheese.

It seems those eyes are accustomed to disappointment, and we wonder if there are pups secreted away in a den somewhere up the beach. We offer no scraps, and life seems tough for a beautiful animal that has been here for over 4000 years.

18

IN THE SHADOW OF BIG RED – Birdsville, Queensland, 2017

`The Big Red Bash' music gig is held each year at the beginning of July, 30km west of Birdsville in the shadow of Big Red, or Nappanerica as the first Australians call it – the 30m high South West Queensland sand dune – on the edge of the Simpson Desert, the largest parallel sand dune desert in the world.

On the first day, we arrive around midday with our newly-cracked windscreen and smashed driver's window, a legacy of flying blue metal catapulted up from oncoming caravans on a narrow sealed road. It's an enlightening hike to the stage in the afternoon, some here for the iconic setting, others set to 'rock the Simpson'... a ragtag collection of intrepid travellers in assorted rigs and campers, caravans, trucks and buses, tents, swags, annexes and awnings.

Many seem content with listening at a distance, either staying at their camp or sitting within eye-shot in their comfy fold-up chairs, a large viewing screen set to the right of the stage... the entire scene dwarfed by an iconic western back-drop – the famed red dune rising abruptly behind. Late in the day, there's a line of people on the dune ridge, the setting sun silhouettes standing kids and grown-ups, while exuber-ant shouting youngsters jump, tumble and slide in the sand, hurtling down towards the back of the stage and immediately scrambling back to the top, more interested in 'doing' the dune than any music or performer.

On day three we meet travellers from West and South Australia – Tom and Jen, Stewart and Ailsa – both couples with similar trucks and fitouts to ours... although a South African design we've only heard about. That night we share stories round their campfire - tales of the road, South Amer-ica, of teaching and assignments in small Territory schools, of indigenous kids... and of previous Simpson Desert cross-ings in rare 'good seasons' when this same desert was alive with rolling fields of wild flowers - their last trip "taking 9-days instead of the normal 5 due to the boundless photo opportunities"... and of finally reaching the top of Big Red, to gaze down on the flat sand pan where we now sit. But instead of the unrelenting sand, they see water as far as the eye can see.

That night the fire crackles, the slightest movement from us or passing foot traffic stirring up dust. We all gaze up at the stars, the clear black sky... just a myriad of stars that sparkle, the astral haze of the Milky Way the only cloud.

With The Bash over, we choose a late start, the early exit ques lengthy, the smell and clatter of diesel engines, the dust clouds thick, but us in no hurry to join the fleeing throng. The empty plain looks flat, unrelenting, dry and desolate, the sun already hot, Big Red brooding. We look at each other and wonder at the almost mythical changes we've only heard about. There is red dust in our nostrils, dust on our clothes and our skin, on our feet and in the corners of our eyes. Heaven help anyone suffering from hay fever or asthma. Our tent and truck are full of red dust. And we try to imagine just last year, 'The Bash' site flooded, and the annual event forced to the Birdsville showgrounds.

And we ponder the possibility of clouds here, heavy grey skies, thunderstorms and spikes of lightning, this same place after days of torrential, unrelenting rain. And our now dusty camp under a metre of water where our newest friends sailed kayaks – right here – in the shadow of Big Red.

19

IT'S ALL ABOUT KARMA – The Coorong, South Australia, 2017

Problems? More like inconveniences really. Busy right up to our departure, leaving late, we have forgotten some bits and pieces. And then there was the matter of a faulty cruise control patched up on the way here.

Well, it has now been a week since leaving Melbourne and this morning we're camped at 42-mile Crossing, The Coorong. A young couple approach after our breakfast of muesli, fruit toast and coffee; Rani and Rasheed French born, with family from the south of India. They are driving a clapped-out camper they have bought in Perth. The inside lights have been left on, the battery now flat. Rani looks sheepish. "Would you have jumper leads?"

We shuffle the truck alongside their van, happy to help out, connecting the leads and wait till their engine kicks in. They talk a little, of their life in France and leaving their jobs to come to Australia on a 12-month visa, wondering what their family would think of their "reckless abandon".

We wish them well, and hope they enjoy their time in our favourite city/home – Melbourne – when they finally reach there. But now we are running late, losing time we can ill afford, our Kangaroo Island ferry connection booked for 1pm. We are 10min from the listed ferry departure time, with a 30-minute check-in period recommended. The phone rings. "You're how far away? 10-minutes? No problem, come on down." We are waved past the wharf barricade, backing the truck on-board, the barricade closed, the bow raised and shut.

Once on Kangaroo Island, we head for Pennington Bay to be greeted by a private show, over 30-dolphins surfing turquoise waves. Then it's on to our camp for the night, us alone among rolling hills, by a secluded river outlet and beach called Western River Cove... and a magnificent Indian evening meal of 'Southern Pepper Curry' served with a glass of selected red from a well-travelled wine cask.

Yes, it seems our luck has changed.

20

JUST A MATTER OF TIME – Adelaide, South Australia, 2013

I am in Adelaide, startled as the nurse draws the curtain behind me, the click of the rings on the rail loud in the quiet of the ward; the sweet smack of cough mixture wafts through the room. I turn away from Sally, my long-time neighbour having a tough time but recovering well. First it was her heart, then a fall; hence the hospital.

Hedley is the old-timer in the next bed, and I have him tagged as the classic `Aussie battler'. His eyes are half closed, his breathing laboured. He lay coughing as the nurse tucks in his sheets with a quick glance across the bed to Sally. The nurse's look is sombre and Sally tugs at my shirt sleeve and whispers; nodding in Hedley's direction. "Don't worry, he'll be glad of the company… and anyway… I have a magazine." I turn and take a step closer to Hedley.

"Been to India young fella?" he asks softly. I detect a smidgin of sing-song Welsh, and answer yes – he's been talking to Sally – I had lived there for a short time. Hedley slowly eyes me up and down, and adjusts the tubes taped to his arm.

Hedley was based down south; in Cannanore, Kerala. "Left in '47," he says. I try a quick calculation, and there is a weak smile from Hedley. "Yeah, that's right. I'll be 84 this year."

"It was God's Own Country in those days young fella; a tropical paradise. We drank whisky and played cricket; me with the best reverse sweep in the business. Renowned for my timing I was. Dropped down to Cochin for R and R sometimes; the beaches, the fishing and Portuguese food. And those Indian women… such beautiful smiles."

Hedley looks down at his taped arm, but his thoughts are definitely somewhere else. "You know young fella, it's funny the things you remember. I'll tell you something about timing." There's a whimsical smile on Hedley's weary face while he gathers his thoughts.

"Can you imagine it? I'm 17, and I'm in India of all places! I'm sitting by a bench stall under an umbrella in Cochin, minding my own business, drinking cold lime juice at 10 in the morning. Well, there's a commotion not far away; I hear whistles and wait for the riot that doesn't happen. I'm curious and enter the throng. And then I see him, with a bright scarlet turban and a wild moustache, standing in the dead centre of things." Hedley's gasping for breath now, and I wait.

"Now…our man, he's an enterprising fella; not like those

other lazy beggars lounging about the place." Hedley thinks for a moment. "You know, it seems this went on every single day?" It is more a statement than a question. "It began each morning with three short, sharp bursts on a small pea whistle he kept in the top pocket of his white kurta. Very clean sort of fella. They'd all come running from the fish markets and stalls."

Hedley's breath is wheezy, but he soldiers on. "In the ensuing bedlam, our man leans on his wooden crutch and juggles something squarish, small and brown; like those opera binoculars. A 3D stereoscope viewer thing, American I think, must have been from the `30s."

"Now, our man had a filmstrip too; 14 grotty black and white pictures of the Taj Mahal. Would you believe it? He keeps that crowd at bay with a ferocious look while taking a coin from the first customer; a big wiry chap. God knows how our man juggles everything. The chap takes the viewer. Our man glares at the crowd, and they give the chap some space."

"Our man leans on his crutch, his good hand free. He pulls something from his fakir cloth bag. It's a small egg-timer; sands in the looking glass sort of thing. He tips it up. And what do you think happens?" After spending time in India I don't even hazard a guess. Hedley continues. "He blows that whistle of course."

"The chap's time starts now and he lifts the viewer to his eyes with one hand, turns towards the morning sun and peers inside the eye pieces." Hedley pauses for a breath. "All hell breaks loose in the jostling crowd. With his other hand, the chap presses a lever at the bottom. That pulls the strip of pictures through the viewer."

"Our man does his best to keep the excited crowd off the chap and before long there's another whistle. Our man takes the viewer from the chap, and the whole thing starts again." This is the brightest Hedley has looked during my entire visit.

"You know young fella, our man held the timer like this!" Hedley grasps an empty specimen bottle up to his eye. "Almost blind I think, poor old codger. He'd watch it like a hawk for 30 seconds, and then out would come that whistle."

"Wonderful to see; checked him on this." Hedley has an ancient timepiece on top of his bedside cabinet. He nods his head from side to side as if still in denial that it ever happened. "That man's timing was absolutely faultless! One blow on that whistle, and the chap's time was up!"

Sally is back home the next week, with me about to leave my 2-cats and head off for a while. I ask how she's going, but can tell she's doing well. There's a film later today, and Majong tomorrow.

"Mind the animals? Why of course," Sally answers without hesitation. She looks as bright as a pin, having just returned from coffee with her step-sister. "And Hedley?" I ask. Her frown says it all. "Not so good" she mumbles.

21

LOCAL INFO RULES. OK? – Cooktown, Far North Queensland, 2017

From the Daintree and Cape Tribulation we drive up the iconic Bloomfield Track to Cooktown, our plan to then head directly north to Cape Melville on our roundabout route to Cape York – until today that is – but as always, we've wondered about the condition of the roads, and it's not until here in Cooktown where we finally get the low-down... the good oil... the truth about the actual situation on the ground up there at Melville.

Jane works at the Tourist Information Centre and cafe, just by the Botanical Gardens, and is eager to help with a wealth of advice after having been in The Gulf regional health field for many years. She scratches her head, tilting her head to one side. Jane seems to recall a possible problem with our plan. "Well it's like this", Jane says. "You just can't beat local info... and I do remember... something." She screws up her eyes in deep thought, deferring to a tall visitor in khaki sitting on the veranda.

"Yeah", the man says, tweaking the wide, warped brim of a lopsided Akubra that's seen more than its share of Gulf weather, "it's been pretty damn wet up there for this time of year, even Park rangers haven't been in yet." He shakes his hatted head. "In fact there's someone stuck out there right now." He nods knowingly, seems to be talking more to himself now. "Had to get a chopper to lift those blokes out. Mmmm... up here for a boys' weekend." His smile is a thin smile. "A pretty expensive exercise that, 'specially since they should never have been up there in the first place." We thank him and Jane for the info, and order Jane's zucchini chocolate cake and 2-flat whites, our maps, booklets and pamphlets in piles on the table.

It is true we have our GPS, hard-copy maps, phones, internet and iPad. But we definitely get the picture. Up here, we are learning that things can get sticky at the drop of a grotty Gulf hat, and it's local knowledge that wins every time.

22

LOOKING FOR MR GOODLUCK – Seven Emu, Northern Territory, 2017

From Hells Gate we drive 4hrs west across the Northern Territory border via the Savannah Way – part of Australia's National Highway One – although here mostly a red dirt and dust road of sand holes, bulldust and corrugations. The turn-off is a 25km track to 'Seven Emu', a sprawling Gulf station of 1665 square miles right on the Robinson River... and a unique partnership with the Australian Wildlife Conservancy.

Our Camp is perched on 30m red cliffs high above the Robinson, a favoured haunt of saltwater crocodiles, two 4m beauties making an appearance in the first hour. Later we gaze down on metre long queenfish that cruise towards the river mouth bounded by distant dunes on a wild Gulf coast. For most of the day the wind moans through white cyprus pines and the afternoon sun throws a shimmering silver sheen over tussled river ripples. At night we listen to the ratchet drone of crickets, the splash of feeding fish, the cries of night birds and the crackle of the campfire – not a skerrick of wind now, and a never-ending magic carpet of stars. The air is cool after another 35degC winter day, the fire's smoky smell loaded with the perfume of dust and dry wood. The old stockmen facilities are rustic... a flat iron roof on round wooden posts, a long drop toilet with sunset river views, and a 44-gallon rusted drum 'donkey' fire-fed heater for luxurious hot showers.

The owner of Seven Emu is Frank, a Gulf country Garawa man in his early 60s, with a knowing black face, the wispy line of a moustache and white hair under a tussled black hat with wide Gulf brim. The blue shirt is of a Wrangler Western check, the worn jeans of faded denim, the slip-on shoes tarnished and dusty. And Frank's a man who doesn't seem to miss anything, has a mischievous streak, his sharp eyes brown, narrowing now and then as if sizing up his audience. I ask about his dad, who bought this place, and Frank screws up his eyes, thoughtful as he remembers his father. "You know, the best advice he gave me was to always talk to the boss when doin' business... keep low and stay out of trouble."

I'm also interested in Ludwig Leichhardt, the famed German botanist/explorer who came this way in the 1840s, naming 'Seven Emu' after a successful hunt, before disappearing without a trace on the return journey. Frank nods. "Yeah... lot's come here interested in that bloke. Good man I reckon. Never shot a blackfella, and asked them about the animals, plants, and the lay of the land."

Later we take a rough, winding track in Frank's battle-worn Land Cruiser ute, out to the old place across sandy ruts, bumps and dried-out crossings, the homestead paddock deserted now due to a lack of reliable water. Frank parks his truck and we make our escape from the searing midday sun... to a grand stand of mangoes reminiscent of a giant cathedral, tall thick columns of trunks, their canopies melding as one. Their shady shroud hangs cool and restful over what is left here, some tumbled-down shed walls, some crooked asbestos sheeting and the overgrown remains of his mum's vegetable garden.

Frank talks fondly of his mother, caring for the family and that vegie garden, but dying at only 61 years old. He points to one particular tree. "See that tree? I was born under that one." He tells a story of his dad leaving home, riding over 500km east to the Queensland frontier Gulf town of Normanton, with a young Frank in tow and his mum left home with a brand new baby. "Yeah, long way that trip, me just a baby." He smiled. "To give me mum a rest dad said. And with me just startin' to walk, reckon he should have got father of the year!"

Our host points to a depleted pond surrounded by scrub just below the paddock and we amble down to the water's edge. It's been a good wet season he says. Frank stoops down to pick up a handful of wet sand, holding it up and gazing intently at the palm of his hand. "In the old days, there were bugs and bait in this sand." Frank frowns. "But nothin' much happenin' now." He falls quiet for a moment as a gust of wind rustles the mango leaves. He tugs at the brim of his hat with one hand, tossing the sand over the water with the other. "And, when the sand hit the surface the fish would always be comin' to the top back then... to see what was happenin'. These days, nothin' much goin' on there either."

I look at the pond, both of us thinking the same thing – there are tadpoles in the water after all, so is that not a good thing? But Frank has been down this road with tourists before. "Cane toads," he says with a hint of contempt, then moves on to another story; when his brother and him encountered a giant crocodile. "He was a big one that saltie, maybe 6m or so... an old one for sure." His eyes follow along the sand bank where we stand. "We was camped on a bank, my brother and me, and this big fella rushed up with his mouth open. Lots of teeth." There's a smile from Frank, then a nervous cough. "Scared the hell out of us. Right between us he went, then just keeled over, dead. We found 20-toads in his belly." We look at each other, then at Frank, more than a little depressed.

Frank is sad at what has happened to this country, the introduction of pests that degrade the land, from assorted weeds to South American cane toads, feral cats and camels, after 65,000 years the current neglect to care for the land. But he is grateful for his good luck too, the Seven Emu pastoral lease purchased in 1953 by his visionary father, an Aboriginal, self-made, self-educated man with no entitlement to vote back then, and Indigenous Australians not granted full citizenship rights until 1968.

By all accounts Frank's father was an exceptionally hard worker, a horse trader and cattle drover with a plan, striking it lucky by winning some money "on the horses", raising 11-kids and insisting they be formally educated, Seven Emu being the only pastoral land lease ever purchased by an Australian Aboriginal.

Frank smiles from the corner of his mouth, and his brown eyes sparkle. "You know what?" He leaves me no time to answer. "It's not always just about good luck. You have to work at stuff I reckon. My old dad lived till his 90s, and always said that I needed to take care of country... that city fellas like you would arrive one day and pay me money to tell stories and show them around."

23

LOST AND FOUND – Cape Arid, Western Australia, 2013

The truck bumps from side to side, the wheels in deeply rutted tracks. Nearer our coastal camp, scrub turns to woodland and we both lurch to the left as we drop a gear and edge across a scary slab of sloping granite. Back on sand, it's our final descent to a wild coast of dazzling white dunes and granite outcrops; down through patches of Yate and Paperbark to reach our secret grove, the tent and truck tucked in clumps of Banksia. Giant Cycads are prehistoric plants, remnants of 200 million years past, the first seed-bearing plants on earth. We are in the wilds of Cape Arid; a vast 280,000Ha National Park on the southeast coast of Western Australia. My girlfriend passes the water bottle, and we stare up at the foreboding mass of Mt Arid, the late afternoon sun catching the bouldered spine of that ancient ridge. We've seen no one for two days now. There are few signs, no power – and true to name – no drinking water.

The next day I trudge 2km uphill from camp to the old homestead site `Hill Springs'; the 4WD track hand hewn with shovel, pick and crowbar. I am told the grave may be somewhere here, and find it 200m to the east. The grave is a parched tussock of grass by a sunken mound; and a crumpled Coke can. Shading my eyes, I gaze up and down the deserted coast as far as the eye can see, then across at the silent, shimmering form of my neighbour; Mt Arid. On the ground the can is an odd faded shade of lipstick pink; the words on the headstone difficult to read: "*To Strive To achieve To leave a splendid memory.*"

I swipe biting March flies from my hands, flicking one to the ground and stomping the voracious beast with the heel of my dust-laden boot. Something makes me turn. I'm being watched it seems – and I freeze – my agitated movement attracting a curious visitor at the edge of the scrub.

The emu is 5m away, 2m tall, silent and watching; neck stretched upward, head turned slightly side on. I feel no sense of danger. The eye is round, of the deepest brown, set in a wizened face of charcoal. The beak is grey and crooked, bent downwards. The front of the neck and side of the head are bare and pale. The animal is panting in the heat, the throat painted with a hint of blue. The feathers on its head are a straggly mess, black, windswept and wild; at the top of the beak, tiny upswept tufts. It is suddenly gone.

My gaze drops to the grave. I am told the old man was a farmer from Balladonia – 200km to the north – selling up and leaving when his only brother died. He travelled alone, by horse and dray, settling in a deep valley east of here. He never married, grew vegetables and hay; ran cattle and sheep.

I breathe in the hot air that rises from the ground. The dust sticks to my face, the silence somehow heavy. Even the flies have fled the heat. Dragging my eyes from the headstone, I peer back over my shoulder, turn and leave the grave for Hill Springs across the way. He would sometimes drop by for breakfast, hiking the 5km across country from his place, proudly declaring to his son-in-law that a sunrise had never found him in bed.

Crossing the track, I find what is left of the homestead and peer down the valley to the sea. I imagine the grass green, the old man's daughter and son-in-law having followed him to these parts and built this homestead; their little piece of heaven.

There was once a post and wire fence, off to the left, bisecting a stand of leaning Cycads; the fence leading to a central iron gate to keep a rooster and foraging brown hens. There was a lean-to kitchen of stone, a smaller hearth and steel flue; the homestead proper being a simple rectangular gable of timber and galvanized iron. Black pigs browsed at the base of the living room hearth; a large sow and seven piglets. There were cows and ducks, fruit trees and vegetables in patchwork tilled paddocks of red loam. Just outside the fence, the fold of a valley led gently down to the ocean. But all I see is a valley parched and brown; ending in a half-moon crescent – shining white in the summer sun – the distant coast of a turquoise Ferret Bay. On the southern horizon lay a colder blue; The Bight and the hundred islands of Recherche Archipelago.

With the old man's health ailing, he was bought here to the homestead for nursing. See a doctor? He had no time for such things. With a boat arriving at Ferret Bay, the old man was too ill to be moved and died in his daughter's arms. Beside me are only ruins, what is left of a kitchen and fireplace, the owners driven out by loneliness, once the old man died, everything left to burn in the horrific fires of the 1920s.

In the morning we head north to Mt Ragged, then on to Balladonia; the track here dead straight and corrugated, changing from soft sand and potholes to limestone outcrops. A flock of eight emu appears from nowhere and glides alongside before suddenly darting away and back into the surrounding stands of Mallee. The air conditioning's on full, air vents shut tight, but the dust gets everywhere.

It's still over 100km to Balladonia when I peer in the rear-view mirror, a billowing dust cloud trailing far behind; like the terrible fires that swept through these parts but could never quite erase 'the splendid memory' of one hardy old man.

24

LOST ON ROOT HOG ROAD – Ophir, New South Wales, 2017

Well... maybe we are not *really* lost... not technically anyway. We are in New South Wales and it is a mere 20km from the old ghost town of Ophir to Hill End – as the crow flies – Ophir once a thriving frontier town and the site of Australia's first 'payable' gold strike. We leave at noon, after a 2-hour bush hike among the long-abandoned diggings and shafts. In the beginning, we take the tamely-named Freemantle Rd. It is dirt, but in good enough nick. And the hard copy map shows a continuing track, the trouble being we are now facing a 'No through road' sign, and our iPad shows the road stopping dead at Macquarie river... which as it happens is a significant piece of water.

Eventually we come to a fork in the road, and stop. One leg heads in the general direction of the river. We check our iPad again, and the truck GPS - the GPS with a river crossing. But yes, this fork does 'head' for the river. But what happens when we get there remains a mystery.

A pick-up ute comes from the opposite direction, a wet stock dog in the back. I wind down the window once the dust settles, the cheery driver "born and bred in these parts". Will we be able to get across the river? The local scratches his chin and looks over our truck. His dog barks and wags his tail. "Yeah... dog's been for a swim just now, and you'll make it in that. Track's a bit rough, rocky in bits... and the farmer doesn't like shooters, so sometimes shuts the gate."

A trip we expected to take an hour, takes over three; hindsight a great thing. But there is definitely something ominous about a fork in the road, when the way forward is a crooked, wooden post with a sign that says `Root Hog Road'.

25

MANTA MAGIC – Lady Elliot Island, Queensland, 2017

The Australian mainland is somewhere 80km away to the west of here, a line of horizontal cloud sitting low over a blue strip of pale sky sandwiched above a wine dark sea. The waning orange sun is sinking and 2-yachts bob just offshore, their masts bouncing to and fro. We are here for 3-days on this tiny island, one of Australia's 19-World Heritage listings, having left the truck at Bundaberg Aerodrome and flown for 45-minutes to this most southerly tip of The Great Barrier Reef. Distant surf roars away to the east, the far side of the island, the early evening air here awash with the clatter of white-capped noddies tussling for evening roosts on wispy branches of bull oak and within jungle clumps of octopus bush, pandanus and pisonia. Waves burst like champagne bubbles at our wet sandaled feet, on banks of pure coral sand as white as snow, the smell of rain sweet on black clouds overhead.

Later we circumnavigate this tiny but lush tropical island on foot and in the dark, hoping to glimpse the last of this season's turtle hatchlings and their newborn dash for the water... on an island once denuded of all topsoil, including almost every stick of vegetation in the destructive quest for fertilizer left by generations of seabirds, that like the turtles, return to breed here year after year.

Our days are spent snorkelling with turtles, sharks, eagle rays, and a myriad of fish. Out by Lighthouse Bommie the water is clear, 15m deep and warm at 23degC. We can't believe our luck and are treated to quite a show: giant dancing manta rays, the gentle giants with black, bat-like wings 3m across, and weighing in at 1-tonne each. They wheel and turn, roll, rise and fall – magic worthy of the Bolshoi Ballet.

26

MEMORIES ON A MOUNTAIN – Mount Alexander, Victoria, 2016

We head north of Melbourne on the Calder for an hour, at the start of this southern Spring. It is the town of Kyneton for coffee, and baguettes for later. Another half hour and we leave the apple orchids of Harcourt Valley and drive towards the farming hamlet of Sutton Grange, then off again northward to the mountain where our truck grinds upwards, and where we finally pull over to the side. A tartan, rubber-backed blanket is spread over a mammoth granite slab, our sitting spot framed by trees with scars of black; their burned bark a reminder of savage summer infernos from years gone by, rushing up from 350m below, those same rolling plains now a painted panorama of pastoral green.

Television towers cast shadows over us, straddling grey eucalypts and grey ragged boulders; shadows the Jaara Jaara folk never saw as they sought out tucker of Black Wallaby, ringtail or Eastern Grey. There is a shimmer in the leaves, the breeze slight and from the south, the smells all eucalyptus and earthen. They called this place `Lanjanuc', those first people; a 370 million year-old granite and bush-covered outcrop, a sacred place of solace and observing their ancient but suddenly changing world.

In our world, the late lunch baguettes are welcome: of eggplant, chicken and crusty French bread. It's 12degC, the sun warm on our backs, Bendigo somewhere to the north. It's getting late when we head onwards and downwards, but there's something else here to see: something odd and strangely out of kilter.

We follow the western slopes south, white cockatoos and corellas grazing in a paddock; sidling past sprawling orchards of apple and pear. Then on a red, rutted dirt track once more up, in the north-west foothills now, classic Australian bush both sides. Until just ahead there's a change, no Manna, Wattle or Box just here; and not the ubiquitous dark spread of plantation Pine.

These trunks are tall and straight, the sweeping bows wide and still winter bare, while on the ground lay a wild crossbreed jungle of suckers that defy the last of winter, a riot of large green leaves – classic Oak. So, this is `The Oak Forest' – the 20-acre, planting a mix of Algerian, bristle-tipped,

English and cork. Planted in 1900, there were grand plans to use the acorns in the leather tanning industry.

Staring back down the hill, the truck sits silent at the bottom of the track in the last of afternoon sun and surrounded by a forest more in keeping with Medieval Europe than in the walkabout wilds of Central Victoria. We are 150km north of Melbourne now, an Antipodean-European city just 180 years old.

27

NEVER SMILE AT A CROCODILE – Lakefield, Far North Queensland, 2017

Some years' ago when visiting East Timor, I asked a silly question. I recall the kids looking temporarily perplexed, a frown replacing their normal smiling countenance. Crocodiles? "Yes of course mister, they are here in our swimming holes. But when they come, we get out of the water."

It was in the Kimberley of West Australia when we next experience the saltwater croc – or the almost-affectionately labelled `saltie' – one cruising right past our chartered yacht 1km out at sea, and others coming inland with the mighty 12m tides, forcing us to flee from sublime rock pools in our motorised dingy back to the safety of our yacht lying just off-shore. But now we are lucky to be in Far North Queensland – Lakefield National Park – having travelled over 500km since that first warning sign... a simple sandwich board sitting on the Cardwell Beach promenade. *'WARNING - ACHTUNG - Recent crocodile sighting in this area'*. And today we've finally seen our very first Queensland saltie, here at Catfish Billabong, Lakefield, the second largest park in Queensland, and as always up here, with brightly-coloured warning signs, and reports of recent nearby saltie sightings. This specimen is only 1.5m, sort of cute and seemingly fast asleep in the mid-day sun, on a nice flat rock overlooking a placid Monet pond of white waterlilies with yellow centres. But it's sure hard to imagine this baby beastie warrants the ubiquitous warnings:

- *Crocodiles inhabit this area – attacks may cause injury or death.*
- *Keep away from the water's edge when launching or retrieving boats.*
- *Do not clean fish or fish waste near the water's edge.*
- *Camp well away from water.*

But I guess it goes without saying: Never... ever... smile at a crocodile; or at least never get close enough to see those teeth.

28

ON A MACASSAN BEACH – East Arnhem Land, Northern Territory, 2017

The beach is windswept, white sand and red rock shelves, the sun burning, the smell of baked earth and newly-burned grass, the early September temperature around 37degC. The walk is a loop, the site recently subject to a regular indigenous 'cool burn to keep down the understorey and to better see these pictures that lay on the ground; outlines built of small red rocks in the 1890s by Aboriginal Yolngu elders And this story could have been lost to future generations, the story of a way of life that existed for hundreds of years and a local connection with the outside world; the Indonesian collection and trading of sea cucumber – or 'trepang' – along with the turtle and pearl shell, all in turn to be traded to the far-off Chinese.

We walk in a clockwise direction, observing the Yolgnu artist's work, an important historical record of visitors to this shore called 'Macassans', from the Indonesian island of Makassar, pictures of their boats and stone houses, of their fireplaces for boiling the trepang.

The Macassan sailors came each December with the monsoon winds, sailing their tri-mast vessels the 1600km journey and taking 2-weeks. They would set up camp at their stone houses by tamarind trees planted on previous visits as location markers, returning home with the corresponding southeast trade winds. They did business with local clans and in exchange for Yolngu labour, and the use of their land, the Macassans traded canoes, metal knives, axes, spears and fish hooks, along with glass and tobacco. Several Yolngu visited Indonesia, returning to East Arnhem the following year.

We follow the marked walking track from the stone outline of a Macassan sailing vessel to that of a Macassan stone house, and wonder at the march of progress. The last Macassan visit was in 1907; 'the last' due to an Australian edict to introduce licenses and taxes payable in Darwin before any trade, the direction of the winds making sailing to Darwin impossible.

29

PLATYPUS PLAYTIME – Eungella, New South Wales, 2017

From Capricorn Caves, we drive to Eungella National Park and pull into Broken River camp just before sunset, Eungella being 100km west of Mackay. Although 26degC today, at 900m elevation it gets cold at night, the mountain rainforest dense, with a lush fern and palm understorey. It is often wet underfoot here, especially at night and early morning. And yes, there is the occasional leech. But for a National Park camp as special as this and with only 12-camping spots, it's a surprise to see only three occupied... and no-one directly on the river bank. There is a little mud, but we do have gumboots and drive right in, our truck bonnet perfectly placed overlooking the river.

We have read about this place some time back, 'the best chance to see platypus in the wild', but to be honest, we take that claim with a grain of salt as neither of us have ever seen a platypus in the wild. So it is incredible to believe our luck when we jump out of the truck to look down on the river and immediately spot a platypus cruising in our direction, seemingly oblivious of our rapturous attention while focused on his evening meal, followed by another of his brethren swimming just upstream.

With the fading light and dinner all done, we listen to a last kookaburra chorus and the white noise of water rushing over rocks upstream, donning jackets as darkness settles, the air dank and earthy, the forest leaves already wet. We sit reading under our truck awning and ponder our luck, just how the hell we managed to pull up, park and be immediately treated to a personal visit from an emblematic oddity and a national treasure normally considered so 'solitary, shy and difficult to observe'.

30

PRIVATE WARS – Melbourne, Victoria, 2013

I met Becky in the supermarket dairy aisle; a vivacious 40-something, born and raised locally. I have seen her around, but had never met before Ed reappeared. I asked how my old friend was. "Not so good," she said. "Still can't sleep… and he really struggles with ANZAC Day. He won't see a doctor. I'm hoping he'll finally talk to other Vets." Becky stared blankly at the shelves of milk. "What else can I do? I love that man." A self-conscious smile and she turns away. I head home thinking of Ed and the upcoming old-soldier reunions across Australia and New Zealand.

Ed is an old school friend, us both from the other side of town. With the coming of conscription, I missed 'The Draft' by one day, gravitating toward anti-war rallies and well-stacked, skinny girls in tight jeans and tees. Ed had wandered up north, picking fruit at first, then somehow ending up in Sydney. Next thing I heard, he had joined the army and gone to Viet Nam. Becky is Ed's wife number 3, of 4-years now.

That night I readied my clothes for an early morning start, Ed having asked me to join him for the annual ANZAC Dawn Remembrance Service at the Melbourne Shrine. I settle at the computer, and with the bills paid, surf the web searching the ANZAC legend.

In 1914 the Australian Commonwealth had existed for only 13-years, the Prime Minister declaring "If the Old Country is at war, so are we", and the opposition pledging Britain "our last man and our last shilling". Turkey joins Germany, and the Russians convince the Allies to tackle the Turks. British commanders conclude Gallipoli to be "open to landing on very easy terms" and at 2.30am 25th April 1915, the Anzacs land on the Gallipoli shore; some as young as 14 years old. The Turks are ready; the Anzacs cut to pieces, and by 2pm the plan has failed, resulting in a terrible stalemate for over 8-months, the British finally ordering an evacuation.

There is an old photograph and I rub my eyes. The picture is faded black and white, a hairline tear running from top to bottom. There is a young man on the right, his unlined face in soft profile, WW1 heavy jacket and boots, buttoned down collar and pockets. He sits stiffly, slightly side on. A medal hangs from his neck and he holds it loosely in one hand; the other arm around a young lad to the left, sitting on table. The uniformed boy is a soldier miniature of his father, his legs hanging casually against his father's knee. Both faces are close; the boy engrossed and gazing down at his father's medal. The father's eyes are covered, with black eye patches. I wonder what he is saying, this casualty of Gallipoli.

In bed I have lain awake forever, pondering the morning's city Dawn Service and a 1915 vision of trapped and exhausted young men; the tricks played on soldiers' tired eyes in the half-light of dawn, the shadows, the fear, the death and maiming. Eventually I fall into fitful sleep, my mind awash with diary entries of a ludicrous miscalculated landing and the slaughter of Gallipoli.

The light is dull, the landscape a blur: steep and rocky with thorny scrub. Weary soldiers wait for rollcall, name after name greeted by silence. There are quiet onlookers; once comrades, some dead for days. One has been shot while cooking dinner and falling by the charred remains of his fire. His mug is full of tea that's cold, his biscuits untouched. There are more bodies by the water hole; snipers again. Washing is dangerous, dysentery rife, the stench appalling.

At 7am the call goes out. Waves of young men – grim, ashen-faced, but fine and straight – trudging up the gully towards the ridge, then dropping to a crawl. Shells burst among the incessant roar and the chatter of machine guns. There's shrieking shrapnel, the ear-splitting crack of rifles, the sparks of striking bullets, the screams of the wounded; the desperate shouts for stretchers amidst a Hell of writhing, mangled men. The same return in pieces, ghosts drifting among mangled heaps of muddy wreckage, gullies choked with blood, some are lost, crawling shattered things; others lay still, frozen in grotesque and impossible shapes. One mad ragged creature is smothered with blood; wildly careening down from a murderous smoking ridge. He rushes and kisses all he passes, leaving a splash of blood on each.

With the ANZAC Dawn Service over, I sit with Ed outside a pub. There is beer on a round table cluttered with empties. Ed smokes like a train. I mention the occasion, the first Service I have attended. "Mine too," says Ed, and our eyes meet. I am struggling to keep conversation – Ed's brow furrowed – and I question the `celebration' of such an obvious defeat as Gallipoli. Ed explodes, spitting out a mouthful of beer. "What the fuck does it matter whether we won or lost?" I am shocked, suddenly aware of my still-open mouth. But it's the furious look on Ed's face quickly changing to bewilderment that scares me. He swallows. "Ahem, sorry mate... I mean..." His words trail off to nothing as he looks away. "Yeah, sorry; never could face these things and wouldn't be here if it wasn't for Becky." He fidgets with the plastic on another pack of smokes.

We sit in silence as a taxi pulls up at the kerb, a young passenger in uniform fumbling with his hat. He throws open the taxi door and a snippet of loud music spills out to where we sit. Ed's face again darkens. The passenger jumps out, dons his hat and stands to attention. He tugs at his brown belt, straightens his jacket and marches past to push through the pub's swinging door.

I know the song well, but just can't place it. Ed looks uncomfortable, sits upright and shoves his chair out from the table, his beer spilling everywhere. "Ah sorry mate", he mumbles, "always hated that bloody song." He is unsteady and wide-eyed as he stands, clearing his throat and wiping his mouth before lurching forward and stumbling off. I grab his jacket from the ground and call out, but he is halfway up the hill.

I finally catch Ed striding out, his eyes downcast. I fall into step with the song circling in my brain. I hear the tune; the chorus coming to me in a flash, the mournful tale of a damaged war vet returning home with no legs. Mmm yes, I understand. Would there be a single Australian who would not know *that* song?

`And the Band Played Waltzing Matilda'

31

UP A MAGIC MOUNTAIN – Lord Howe Island, New South Wales, 2010

Under a canopy of mountain palms, primeval smells of black mud and musty rainforest drench the air. Sphagnum moss smothers stunted trunks with bright green velvet, while moorei orchids cling to rotting stumps in an understorey of lichens, staghorns and more than 30-species of fern. In this mystical remnant of a place, we tramp prehistoric paths along a wet, silent, leaf-littered floor. My boots squelch, then slip on rock or slimy tree roots. Ducking under a branch, a shroud of old-man's-beard lichen tickles my face. Beetles found nowhere else on earth scurry about on their business.

Palm fronds litter the burrows of sooty terns that will return tonight to find luminous glow-in-the-dark fungi, irresistible to snails and slugs.

In this 40ha cloud forest, where steamy drifts waft among a gloomy moss-laden world, I could be on New Zealand's South Island or lost in the Peruvian Andes. Yet I look down from this magic mountain to a turquoise lagoon far below, bounded by a long dazzling beach and a sea pounding on the teeth of the planet's most southerly coral reef.

A sudden rustle and low resonant purrs from nearby undergrowth announce the arrival of the world's rarest bird. Woodhens are without tails, about 35cm long, olive-brown with rufous banded wings. This pair has claimed about 2ha; in days gone by, they would have risked certain death by seeking us out. Like the NZ kiwi, with no predators they lost the ability to fly many generations ago. Curiosity satisfied, they nonchalantly scratch at our feet for worms, small invertebrates and insect larvae, tossing dead leaves aside with long curved beaks.

We are on NSW's Lord Howe Island atop Mt Gower, after clambering 875m up from sea level through palm forests. We have hugged ancient cliff-faces, trodden rock-crowded creek beds, hoisted ourselves by rope up impossible goat trails, and struggled for breath and footholds to reach this silent Eden at the southern end of the island. Just a 2-hour flight from Sydney, this World Heritage-listed island – at 11km by 1.8km at the widest point – has only one indigenous mammal: a bat. Five bird and more than 50-plant species occur nowhere else on the planet. Eighty million years ago, the territory was part of Gondwanaland, and six million years ago a volcanic eruption created the island.

Even intrepid Polynesian mariners did not venture here; the earliest arrivals came in 1788 on a ship that brought the first colonists to mainland Australia. The holds were filled with turtles and palm hearts to feed the starving mainland colonists; the first permanent residents 3-Englishmen and their families from NZ in 1834, farming meat and vegetables for the burgeoning whaling industry. American whalers arrived from Sag Harbor, San Francisco and Nantucket to hunt the middle ground. Goats and pigs were purposely let loose, as were cats and mice. The seabirds, pigeons, parrots and woodhens were hunted and, having never known humans, were easily clubbed and shot, their eggs and young taken. Plants, roots, tubers, grubs and insects were destroyed, with 9-bird species soon extinct.

A shipwreck in 1918 unleashed swarms of black rats; our guide Dean telling us a war has raged ever since, with 13,771 killed in 1927 alone. In 1922 the Tasmanian masked owl was introduced to take up the battle but took a liking to the remaining native birds. With the whalers gone, the mainland authorities raised the question of relocating the islanders, who were obviously destitute, due to their ragged clothes of disused flour bags and goatskin moccasins. There was melaleuca tea, geranium-leaf smoking tobacco, and a heady alcohol brewed of wild figs and banana skins. Homes were simple rectangular structures, walled and gable-roofed with palm-frond thatch.

The mainland government surveyor noted the islanders'

diet: garfish, salmon, rock cod, turtles, seabirds, eggs, sweet potato, peach pies, butter, milk and maize and an abundance of pig and goat. He deemed their removal unnecessary. No wealthy 1920s European home was complete without an exotic potted plant and Lord Howe's hardy kentia palm was the most sought after. The islanders were quick to promote a palm-seed industry.

On Mt Gower, the temperature drops and I sense an evil eye. I turn to meet the cold, golden stare of a satin-black currawong with its head cocked sideways, intent on stealing my thoughts. Smaller than its mainland cousins, it lets fly with a strident ringing call. Leg rings tinkle as it shifts its weight from one clawed foot to the other. The descent is more than three hours. Dean, who has been an island ranger for 16-years, points through the mist to the gothic spires of Balls Pyramid, 550m above an unsettled sea. It is a rocky Mont Saint-Michel floating on an antipodean ocean 20km southeast of the primeval forest where we stand.

Below me is a 20m rope we must clamber down; this being the 'Get Up Place'. Wild pigs found this wall impossible to climb to the last haven of the woodhen. Gripping the rope tightly, I smile nervously at my girlfriend as Dean suggests it's best to abseil down the vertical drop. We follow the Erskine Valley to the sound of trickling water, ambling between strange tepee pandanus propping themselves up with a profusion of roots from halfway up their trunks, until we reach another rope, high above boiling seas. We don helmets as a precaution against frequent rock falls from the black volcanic cliffs and gingerly clamber beneath the face of 777m Mt Lidgbird and safely down to a rock and rubble beach.

On our Ebbtide cottage veranda we rest weary muscles, basking in sun filtered through stands of hibiscus, frangipani and the ubiquitous kentia palm. The winter air temperature is a balmy 24C. Green pawpaw orbs covered in droplets from showers hang from a gnarled trunk under a shiny canopy of leaves shaped like hands. At dusk our host drops us at a local restaurant. We dine on freshly caught kingfish tempura and a South Australian Riesling, and then the restaurateur returns us to our cottage, as is polite island custom. With no streetlights and no moon, we marvel at the absence of mobile phones and the far-flung scatterings of the Milky Way.

We soon slumber as returning sooty terns chatter on the breeze, an emerald-winged dove coos and the Pacific ebbs and flows among the rocks of Hells Gate below us. Next morning, we snorkel amid coral, myriad coloured fish and mammoth kingfish at nearby Ned's Beach Sanctuary.

Enroute to the airstrip we stop between tall Norfolk pines at the edge of the village. We talk with our host, Emma, a freckled 30-something mother of two young boys, of mainland restaurants and bright lights, boarding schools and finally of island hospitality. Emma stares out to sea. "Yeah, I was born here," she says. I must look surprised, and she laughs. "In the shadow of that very mountain." She casually waves an arm towards the lagoon and a distant Mt Gower. Palm fronds sway in the breeze, sounding like light rain.

I wonder aloud, "I guess you reach a certain age and an island just isn't big enough; there's a need to see the world."

She shrugs and nods. "And maybe you just wake up and

realise everything was always here, at the foot of that magic mountain."

32

RED DESERT DREAMING – Kimberley, Western Australia, 2013

Strange figures are painted in broad strokes of red ochre – Wandjina spirit-men – eerie round faces with big pools for eyes. I stand next to Maurice, "a Worara blackfella" and a driver at local mines. I ask him why they have no mouths. His voice is hushed, as he points at the staring spaceman figures. "Ah, you see bro, these spirits, they have much magic; so much power. They have no need for mouths." He knows these spirits well. "We must be respectful, 'cause if offended, lightning will strike us dead for sure."

We're at the far northwest of Australia amidst 1000km of

serrated and sunburnt Kimberley coast. This is the edge of a vast moonscape, a coastal escarpment broken by wild inland ranges and 12m tides careering through narrow coastal gorges. I stand in awe of these 30,000yr old spirits that morph before our eyes into animals and fish. This is part of the 'Dreaming', the ancient ongoing story of Maurice's people and the great creator bringing life to a parched earth. Dugongs and turtles mingle with fish, all adrift this rock-face gallery. The air is damp and dusty. The sheer red sandstone shades us from a blistering morning sun. I turn and gaze at the Indian Ocean and down at a great red rock of an island just offshore; a seagoing Uluru afloat a turquoise pond.

Maurice has dishevelled curly hair, his black face round with a low forehead and eyes half-closed as if he's lost in thought. His short-cropped beard is grey. An open-necked khaki shirt reveals rows of horizontal welts; the initiation scars of another world. His shorts are baggy, of sun-bleached blue; his bare feet caked in red dust.

His English is slow and deliberate; his hand movements expressive. In addition to his own tongue, he speaks Ngarinyin and "some Wunambol-Gamberre." I ask him if he's travelled. He says he's been to Perth, over 2000km south. Maurice screws up his nose. "Didn't like it much at that place; no good for me bro. Even the quiet streets, them much too busy." He shakes his shaggy head and looks out to sea. "I miss the colour of the water if I leave here." He turns his head inland. "And I miss the moon on them hills; the sun and the red skies. I miss the songs of the old people that float on the night wind."

The silence is heavy, and I'm loathed to break it. Maurice waits, looks at me knowingly, then follows my gaze back down to the island. "You know bro, the blackfellas in olden days, they learned the secret ways. They paddled on small rafts out there." He points a crooked finger. "They must climb, and stay until they are men." I ponder how the hell anyone climbs 30m vertical walls. "Yes bro; those blackfellas are just kids, and some, they die. There are many sharks here; stingers and salties." He extends both arms out to his sides. I get the picture; the saltwater crocodiles are giants. Maurice's eyes return to his people's faded paintings and I wonder how long this Dreaming can last.

To get here we've left Broome 2-days earlier – my girlfriend and I – on a chartered baronial twin-masted ketch with dark, wood-panelled cabins; accompanied by visiting whales, side-winding sea snakes and curious green and brown turtles turning their heads to stare before plummeting to depths unknown.

At Cape Baskerville we entered Lacepede Channel, the site of a 1935 cyclone sinking 36-pearl luggers and drowning 142; a timely reminder of a wild coast. Our first chilli-red sunset coincided with the appearance of the flashing light of Cape Leveque. My girlfriend stares into the green glow of the radar screen. Are the blips whales or rocks? With the first sun The Buccaneers have emerged from a dark infinity pool; 800 rocky islands of parched pink.

Picking up Maurice at Cockatoo Island, we passed Koolan and moored at Talbot Bay where a lone 3m tawny nurse shark arrived with dusk, cruising around and beneath us, sinuous tail rhythmically flicking from side to side. Another appeared, slipping alongside and under the first. By nightfall there were 6-identical sharks; streams of phosphorous lights trailing behind as the sharks rise to the surface, gracefully criss-crossing each other to the dulcet strains of Debussy's Claire De Lune that waft from the galley where Maurice cooked fettuccini.

In the morning we crossed Collier Bay, passing Kingfisher Islands and landing here at Raft Point. We've clambered across a rubble beach and up past crumbling sea cliffs, grabbing at sticky tufts of spinifex that somehow smell of caramel. We paused in the sparse shade of an ancient boab with a 3m girth.

I take in the odd spirit-men paintings for one last time, stumble down the cliff-face and we leave on an outgoing tide. Passing Montgomery Islands, the 2600Ha reef rises from the ocean floor. The mainsail is unfurled, waking tiny bats that abruptly emerge from the sail into the dazzling sunlight. The startled creatures dart between masts, before settling among stern rigging. The Kingfisher Islands offer up another salient sunset and by nightfall the bats are gone. At Silver Gull Creek we lounge under the stars until ripples and rhythmic breathing alert us to a surrounding pod of dolphins rising, spouting and circling as they round up fish.

Back at Old Broometown we dine among clumps of palms and flickering tea-lights beneath a scented canopy of frangipani and patches of the ubiquitous Milky Way. The beer is cold; the whole-baked threadfin salmon adorned with sprigs of coriander. Later we sit by our B&B pool, the balmy moonlight throwing jungle patterns across the flagstones.

A Kimberley breeze ruffles palm fronds, while my girlfriend unrolls a small painting, The painting was a parting gift from Maurice, while standing at the Cockatoo mine jetty.

It's on handmade paper – burned browns, reds and yellow – the circling shapes friendly spirits engendered by the land. I recall Maurice's sweeping hand movements and his slow drawl. "Even in modern times bro, them spirits, they wander always, in search of the babies to continue the Dreaming."

33

SACRED PANELS –
Yirrkala, Northern
Territory, 2017

We are in Northern Territory on the Gove Peninsula, East Arnhem Land, our destination the airy corridors of the Yirrkala Art Centre: an expansive display of Indigenous Arnhem Aboriginal art. To get to here it's been a drive on the reddest of roads, billowing dust the norm, corrugations common and the occasional rut, '24hrs from Katherine' the information brochure says, although 'only' 700km as our truck flies.

We have overnighted at Mainoru Roadhouse, our recommended stop in accordance with our over-the-counter, no-cost, 10-day permit from the Northern Land Council office in the Katherine main street. On our arrival at Nhulunbuy on the Gove Peninsula, we have sought out the 'Dhimurru

Corporation' office for camping permits on Aboriginal land, then our NT liquor permit to buy take-away alcohol.

The seaside town of Yirrkala is another 20km to the south, the scent of frangipani on a breeze, the sun hot, the Gulf of Carpentaria a glittering turquoise blue and the sand a dazzling white. The gallery is adjacent an Aussie Rules oval of green grass, a stadium/shed and store. Impressive murals cover outside walls... the heros of Aboriginal rights going back to the 1960s. The gallery entry is plain and unadorned, the glass door dark and dusty under a wide, shady verandah.

Once inside is another story... a treasure-trove of hand-made indigenous art typical of this isolated region. There are forests of traditional wooden Yidaki – or didgeridoo – with the most intricate traditional designs, wall hangings and paintings. Shelves are stacked full of books, CDs and carvings. Simple racks are laden with woven bags and a photographer snaps special pieces in a cluttered room off to the side.

Justin is lean, has a greying mane of straight hair and has been here since the 90s. He rises from behind his computer screen, stands tall in a plain white tee shirt and blue jeans. There is something we must see, he says. Out back is a specially built darkened room with timber steps down to a small sunken cellar of sorts, atmospheric with soft lighting designed to highlight 2-vertical panels. Both are intricate in their design, rustic browns and blacks, with a low bench seat directly across from, and in front of the panels. There is a lot for the visitor to take in.

The panels are about 1m wide by 3m high and hang side by side. And they tell an Aboriginal creation story, presented in detail by the Indigenous artists but evidently with no Christian influence, coercion or direction.

Justin tells a story that begins "before my time", the panels created by Yolnu elders and gifted to the newly opened Methodist church in 1963, intended for permanent display as a screen behind the communion table. Justin waves one hand towards the front door. "You would have seen the church over the road."

The story continues... 10-years after the panels are installed, around 1983, a new missionary arrives at the church, saying the panels are inappropriate for a church, and are most certainly "heathen" works. Both panels are taken from inside the church against the wishes of the Parish Committee.

The panels lie neglected and forlorn for 4-years, but are never completely forgotten, propped against an outside wall exposed to the ways of mud wasps and weather, before being rescued by a coalition of Indigenous and non-Indigenous activists and cleaned by the staff of the Australian University.

Justin pauses for effect, and to gather his thoughts while peering over the top of thin-rimmed glasses. "And that was the beginning of a movement here in Arnhem... you might say, the very beginning of the entire Australian Indigenous Land Rights movement."

Down in the cellar my eyes are drawn to the panel on the right, with a small figure top and centre – a diminutive painted bird – this little bird being the ancestral link between the spirit and the temporal worlds, flanked by helpers on his immediate right and left... the cicada and the possum. Alas, an ancient story considered inappropriate to the doctrines taught in a civilized house of worship.

34

SNAKE TALES – Portland, Victoria, 2017

Every now and then we are reminded of exactly where we live, in a `lucky' country blessed with twenty-one of the most venomous snakes on earth... from a list of the top twenty-five. And that's along with a menagerie of deadly fish, sharks, octopus, jellyfish, spiders and crocodiles.

Today we are 150km southwest of Melbourne, on the Great Ocean Road, at the equally iconic Cape Nelson Lighthouse – famous for whale watching, vicious swarms of marauding March flies – and the funky ambiance of Isabella's Cafe. The flat whites are welcome, piping hot and strong, the fresh croissants filled with cheese and sun-dried tomatoes; all enjoyed to the dulcet strains of Simone and Sinatra.

When finally time to go, we ask for directions to the toilets, taking care to close the door when leaving, the local snakes apparently prone to sneaking in and drinking from the toilet cistern.

35

SUNDAY DRIVE TO TURKEY CREEK – Arcturus, Queensland, 2017

There has been lots of rain, the remnants of Cyclone Debbie rending this Queensland track full of waterlogged potholes and a labyrinth of deep muddy ruts. And to make things even more interesting, there's a flying army of nasty, biting midges whenever we dare get out of the truck.

We've come from Agnes Water on the coast, turning off to travel the 'scenic route' - only 20km as the crow flies - the track a winding dashed line on our iPad Hema maps... and it is shown on our truck GPS, so we've decided it really does exist and gone with it. It was odd though, for such a short distance, that the GPS added hours onto our anticipated trip time when we changed from its preferred route to our more 'scenic' pick.

Bumping along for hours now, we dodge tree branches, ruts and flooded potholes as best we can. Amongst the paperbark swamp there's also the occasional creek crossing to deal with, and a local dry detour if we get lucky. For much of the time though, it's best that one of us walks on ahead to test the lay of the land, the depth of water or mud, and give directions. We like to nurse our precious truck as best we can.

There are hazards walking though, the aforementioned midges, my sandaled right foot sinks in a hole of stinking grey mud that sticks like glue... Sue says giving me the appearance of wearing one grey sock. There are also free-range bovine onlookers for the driver to negotiate from time to time, curious mostly, and tending to wander along the track with an air of nonchalant disdain. Just here, there is another bend on this character-building track we have chosen, when almost to the Turkey Beach turnoff... and the white Land Cruiser Workmate ute bogged up to its axles.

Jason and Mack have time off from the mines, with Mack's father running a farm near here. They have not gotten far though, with Mack seeming a little courageous to city slickers like us. In fact he may have chosen the most challenging route from 3-options right here. Nevertheless, Mack is happy to see us, his diff locks not working his recovery gear limited to a snatch strap, and a hydraulic barrel jack that he has somehow managed to prop under the rear axle but is now jammed stuck. He glances up and down the track. "There's not much traffic about these parts." As it happens, we have all the recovery gear, never used till now, and are more than happy to help out, knowing all too well that next time it could be us.

The Land Cruiser ute comes out with a roar, a splash and a spray of mud, leaving Mack's hydraulic jack swallowed by the watery abyss, like some murky, muddy time capsule planted for another thrill-seeking 4WD enthusiast to rediscover years from now.

36

TRIP TO THE TIP – Cape York, Far North Queensland, 2017

We are 500km north of Cairns and heading for the tip of Cape York via Musgrave Roadhouse, Morton and Bramwell Junction, on road corrugations that loosen teeth, across creeks, rivers and dangerous dust holes, while dodging drifts of wandering 'Droughtmaster' cattle. Next it is the famed Jardine Ferry: a motorized, cable driven flat-bottom barge, then on to Bamaga and finally 'The Tip'... an understated title that takes a bit of getting used to. Nevertheless, it is the most northern tip of mainland Australia... right here... where we stand on this wild rocky outcrop. And it really is Torres Strait that lay before us, after 4-months on the road, our most northern mainland frontier, a romantic realm of past explorers and somehow-exotic halfway islands, with Papua New Guinea just across the way.

But we are not alone, this being a pilgrimage of sorts for others that come this way, many seemingly returning home the exact same route in the quickest manner possible... an eclectic gaggle of grey nomads, extended families, friends, loners, clubs and couples. Some have 'Tip' team T-shirts especially printed, in the brightest fluoro colours with their very own meaningful message. Others see it as a test of nerve and a culmination of their 4WD adventure trek – to conquer the iconic Old Telegraph Track – a sort-of coming of age initiation where the toughness of both vehicle and driver are tested, with any subsequent wreckage or scars paraded with pride and bragged about for years to come.

At The Tip today the east wind is fresh on the side of our faces, the air salty, with hot, stinging sun giving way to intermittent drifts of rain. We gaze north across a narrow strait to York Island, past a pod of pilot whales that surface and sink, as they journey east. A gigantic turtle suns itself on the surface and a 4m croc heads west to who knows where.

But the wildlife can wait as we all take turns standing by a rickety sign on a steel post, for the compulsory photo opportunity. 'The T-shirts' toss in a fishing line and pose for additional action snaps. One dad nudges his 4yo son close to the edge for a better photo and barks instructions on how to cast a fishing line... so close that we fear the poor kid may slip in his rubber thongs and tumble into the same heaving water that throws spray onto his tiny feet.

There is no denying the place is special, even with the rain and wind, the constant stream of scrambling souls like us, the whirr of an overhead drone and the whiff of cigarette smoke here and there. It is sad though, to think of someone willingly leaving litter at a place like this; the occasional coke can, plastic drink bottle or butt that threaten to make The Tip 'A Tip'. And it is disappointing to think of those almost anonymous persons travelling from far away while carrying a can of paint to leave their mark on these ancient protruding rocks that have sat here forever, the first Australians leaving them untouched for 65,000 years.

37

WHAT'S IN A NAME? – Broken Hill, New South Wales, 2017

Broken Hill seems a long way from anything, while certainly entrenched in Australian folklore; being the 'BH' component of 'The Big Australian' BHP Billiton, and becoming the first city in Australia to be included on the National Heritage List – the 'broken hill' that gave the town its name being a number of hills that appeared to have a break in them once upon a time. Alas, all have now been mined away.

And there's no shortage of culture here, with at least 8-galleries showcasing the work of iconic Australian artists including Pro Hart and Jack Absolam. The actor Chips

Rafferty and the acclaimed opera singer June Bronhill also came from these parts.

Today the air is dense and hot at 37degC, and we are told we are lucky due to recent temperatures reaching 50degC. But it is hard to warm to a place where over 700 souls have been lost in mining accidents, the youngest killed at age 14 and most streets named after rocks and minerals.

References

All text Copyright © Ian Cochrane 2022

National Library of Australia Cataloguing-in-Publication data: Cochrane, Ian James, 1951

Everything under the Sun – Australian short stories of light and shade from A to Z / Ian Cochrane, 2nd edition p-book, 4th edition e-book

Subjects:

Cochrane, Ian James, 1951

Adventure

People

Places

Roadtrip

Short stories

The human condition

Travel – Australia

Travel – New South Wales

Travel – Northern Territory

Travel – Queensland

Travel – Victoria

Travel – South Australia

Travel – Tasmania

Travel – Western Australia

Cover image: `Under the Sun' Copyright © Ian Cochrane 2022

www.ingramcontent.com/pod-product-compliance
Lightning Source LLC
Chambersburg PA
CBHW070621120726
47909CB00004B/1267